Nan Sherwood's Winter Holidays; Or, Rescuing the Runaways

Annie Roe Carr

NAN SHERWOOD'S WINTER HOLIDAYS

Or, Rescuing the Runaways

by

ANNIE ROE CARR

1916

CHAPTER I

DOWN PENDRAGON HILL

Ta-ra! ta-ra! ta-ra-ra-ra! ta-*rat!*

Professor Krenner took the silver bugle from his lips while the strain echoed flatly from the opposite, wooded hill. That hill was the Isle of Hope, a small island of a single eminence lying half a mile off the mainland, and not far north of Freeling.

The shore of Lake Huron was sheathed in ice. It was almost Christmas time. Winter had for some weeks held this part of Michigan in an iron grip. The girls of Lakeview Hall were tasting all the joys of winter sports.

The cove at the boathouse (this was the building that some of the Lakeview Hall girls had once believed haunted) was now a smooth, well-scraped skating pond. Between the foot of the hill, on the brow of which the professor stood, and the Isle of Hope, the strait was likewise solidly frozen. The bobsled course was down the hill and across the icy track to the shore of the island.

Again the professor of mathematics—and architectural drawing—put the key-bugle to his lips and sent the blast echoing over the white waste:

Ta-ra! ta-ra! ta-ra-ra-ra! ta-*rat!*

The road from Lakeview Hall was winding, and only a short stretch of it could be seen from the brow of Pendragon Hill. But the roof and chimneys of the great castle-like Hall were visible above the tree-tops.

Now voices were audible—laughing, sweet, clear, girls' voices, ringing like a chime of silver bells, as the owners came along the well-beaten path, and suddenly appeared around an arbor-vitae clump.

"Here they are!" announced the professor, whose red and white toboggan-cap looked very jaunty, indeed. He told of the girls' arrival to a boy who was toiling up the edge of the packed and icy slide.

1

Walter Mason had been to the bottom of the hill to make sure that no obstacle had fallen upon the track since the previous day.

"Walter! Hello, Walter!" was the chorused shout of the leading group of girls, as the boy reached the elevation where the professor stood.

One of the girls ran to meet him, her cheeks aglow, her lips smiling, and her brown eyes dancing. She looked so much like the boy that there could be no doubt of their relationship.

"Hello, Grace!" Walter called to his sister, in response.

But his gaze went past the chubby figure of his shy sister to another girl who, with her chum, was in the lead of the four tugging at the rope of the gaily painted bobsled. This particular girl's bright and animated countenance smiled back at Walter cordially, and she waved a mittened hand.

"Hi, Walter!" she called.

"Hi, Nan!" was his reply.

The others he welcomed with a genial hail. Bess Harley, who toiled along beside her chum, said with a flashing smile and an imp-light of naughtiness in either black eye:

"You and Walter Mason are just as thick as leaves on a mulberry tree, Nan Sherwood! I saw you whispering together the other day when Walter came with his cutter to take Grace for a ride. Is he going to take you for a spin behind that jolly black horse of his?"

"No, honey," replied Nan, placidly. "And I wouldn't go without you, you know very well."

"Oh! wouldn't you, Nan? Not even with Walter?"

"Certainly not!" cried Nan Sherwood, big-eyed at the suggestion.

"Only because Dr. Beulah wouldn't hear of such an escapade, I guess," said the wicked Bess, laughing.

"Now! just for that," Nan declared, pretending to be angry, "I won't tell you—yet—what we were talking about."

"You and Walter?"

"Walter and I—yes."

"Secrets from your chum, Nan! You're always having something on the side that you don't tell me," pouted Bess.

"Nonsense! Don't you know Christmas is coming and everybody has secrets this time of year?"

"Hurry up, girls!" commanded the red-haired girl who was helping pull on the rope directly behind the chums. "I'm walking on your heels. It will be night before we get on the slide."

"We're in the lead," Bess flared back. "Don't be afraid, Laura."

"That may be," said Laura Polk, "but I don't want Linda Riggs and her crowd right on top of us. They're so mean. They came near running into us the other day."

"But the professor called 'em down for it," said the fourth girl dragging the bobsled, who was a big, good-natured looking girl with a mouthful of big white teeth and a rather vacuous expression of countenance when she was not speaking.

"He ought to send Linda Riggs and her friends down first," Nan Sherwood suggested.

"No, ma'am!" said Bess Harley, shrilly.

"We're here ahead of 'em all. We can go first, can't we, Professor Krenner?"

"Certainly, my dear," responded the professor. "Look over the sled, Walter, and see that it is all right."

The handsome sled was almost new and there could be nothing the matter with it, Walter was sure. Other parties of girls from the Hall, dragging bobsleds, were appearing now. They were all the bigger girls of the school, for the younger ones, or "primes," as they were designated, had their own particular hill to slide on, nearer the Hall.

Dr. Beulah Prescott, principal of Lakeview Hall, believed in out-of-door sports for her girls; but they were not allowed to indulge in coasting or sleighing or skating or any other sport, unattended. Professor Krenner had general oversight of the coasting on Pendragon Hill, because he lived in a queerly furnished cabin at the foot of it and on the shore of the lake.

He marshalled the sleds in line now and took out his watch. "Three minutes apart remember, young ladies," he said. "Are you going with your sister's sled, Walter?"

"This first time," said the boy, laughing. "Grace won't slide if I don't, although Nan knows how to steer just as well as I do."

"Of course she does," said Bess, with assurance. "We don't need a boy around," she added saucily.

"They're very handy animals to have at times," said the professor, drily. "Wait a bit, Miss Riggs!" he added sharply. "First come, first served, if you please. You are number three. Wait your turn."

"Well, aren't those girls ever going to start?" snapped the tall girl, richly dressed in furs, who had come up with a party of chums and a very handsome "bob."

Professor Krenner was quite used to Linda's over-bearing ways, and so were her fellow-pupils. They made the rich and purse-proud girl no more beloved by her mates. But she could always gather about her a few satellites—girls who felt proud to be counted the intimates of the daughter of a railroad president, and who enjoyed Linda Riggs' bounty.

Not that there were many girls at Lakeview Hall whose parents and guardians were not well off. The school was a very exclusive school. Its course of instruction prepared the girls for college, or gave them a "finish" for entrance upon their social duties, if they did not elect to attend a higher institution of learning.

On this occasion Professor Krenner paid no further attention to Linda Riggs. Walter Mason had already taken his place on his sister's sled at the steering wheel in front, with his boots on the footrests. His sister got on directly behind him and took hold of his belt. Behind her Nan, Bess, little, fair-haired Lillie Nevins, who was Grace's particular chum, and who had ridden over on the sled from the Hall, Amelia Boggs, the homely girl, and Laura Polk, the red-haired, sat in the order named. There were rope "hand-holds" for all; but Grace preferred to cling to her brother. The first trip down the hill was always a trial to timid Grace Mason.

"All ready?" queried Walter, firmly gripping the wheel.

"Let her go!" cried Laura, hilariously.

"And do give somebody else a chance!" exclaimed Linda.

Professor Krenner's watch was in his hand. "Go!" he shouted, and as the red-haired girl's heels struck into the hard snow to start the creaking runners, the old gentleman put the bugle to his lips again and blew another fanfare.

"We're off!" squealed Bess, as the bobsled slipped over the brow of the descent and started down the slippery slide with a rush.

Fifty feet below the brink of the hill a slight curve in the slide around a thick clump of evergreens hid the sled from the group at the top. They could hear only the delighted screams of the girls until, with a loud ring of metal on crystal, the runners clashed upon the ice and the bobsled darted into view again upon the frozen strait.

The first bobsled ran almost to the Isle of Hope before it stopped. By that time Professor Krenner had started the second one, and the impatient Linda was clamoring for what she called her "rights."

"We'll show 'em how to speed a bobsled, if you'll give us a chance," she complained. "That thing of the Mason's didn't get to the island. We'll show 'em!"

Nan Sherwood and her friends piled off the first sled upon the ice with great delight and much hilarity.

"I declare!" gasped Laura. "I left my breath at the top of the hill. O-o-o! What a ride!"

"It's ju-just like swinging too high!" burst out flaxen-haired Lillie.

Nan and Bess had brought their skates slung over their shoulders by the straps. Before getting up off the sled the chums put these on and then were ready to draw the heavy sled back across the ice to the shore.

"Get aboard—all of you!" Bess cried. "All you lazy folks can have a ride!"

"And do hurry!" added Nan. "Here come some more bobs."

The second sled did not gain momentum enough to slide half-way across the strait between the mainland and the Isle of Hope. But now appeared the "Linda Riggs' crew," as Laura called them, and their shiny, new sled. Out of the enveloping grove which masked the side of Pendragon Hill it came, shooting over the last "thank-you-ma'am" and taking the ice with a ringing crash of steel on crystal.

"Got to hand it to 'em!" exclaimed Walter, with admiration. "That's some sled Linda's got."

"So's ours," Bess said stoutly. "See, they're not going to run farther than we did."

"I don't know about that," murmured Nan, honestly.

"Come on!" Bess cried. "Let's get back and try it again. I know those horrid things can't beat the *Sky-rocket*."

The other girls had already piled upon the bobsled. Walter started them with a push and called a "good-bye" after them. He was going to put on his own skates and skate up the strait to the Mason house. The family was staying here on the shores of Lake Huron much later than usual this year.

Nan Sherwood and Bess Harley had no trouble at all in dragging their mates across the ice upon the *Sky-rocket*. Linda's sled, the *Gay Girl*, did go farther than the first-named sled, and Bess was anxious to get to the top of the hill to try it over again.

"It will never do in this world to let them crow over us," Bess declared.

She and Nan slipped off their skates at the edge of the ice and all six laid hold of the long rope to pull the *Sky-rocket* up the hill.

A fourth bobsled rushed past them, the girls screaming and laughing; and then a fifth flew by.

"Mrs. Gleason said she would come over before supper time," Laura Polk said. Mrs. Gleason was the physical instructor at the Hall.

"Let's get her on our sled!" cried Bess.

"Let's!" chorused the others.

But no teacher save Professor Krenner was on the brow of the hill when the *Sky-rocket* was hauled into position again. This time Nan steered, with firmly braced feet, her mittened hands on the wheel-rim, and her bright eyes staring straight down the course.

"Are you ready?" cried the professor, almost as eager as the girls themselves. Then he blew the warning blast to tell all below on the hillside that the *Sky-rocket* was coming.

Ta-ra! ta-ra! ta-ra-ra-ra! Ta-*rat!*

With a rush the sled was off. It disappeared around the evergreen clump. The hum of its runners was dying away when suddenly there sounded a chorus of screams, evidently from the *Sky-rocket* crew. Following this, a crash and a turmoil of cries, expressing both anger and fright, rang out upon the lower hillside.

CHAPTER II

THE FAT MAN WITH HIS GROUCH

Nan Sherwood had steered this big bobsled down Pendragon Hill many times. She had no fear of an accident when they started, although the rush of wind past them seemed to stop her breath and made her eyes water.

There really was not a dangerous spot on the whole slide. It crossed but one road and that the path leading down to Professor Krenner's cabin. At this intersection of the slide and the driveway, Walter Mason had erected a sign-board on which had been rudely printed:

STOP! LOOK! LISTEN!

Few people traversed this way in any case; and it did seem as though those who did would obey the injunction of the sign. Not so a heavy-set, burly looking man who was tramping along the half-beaten path just as Nan and her chums dashed down the hill on the bobsled. This big man, whose broad face showed no sign of cheerfulness, but exactly the opposite, tramped on without a glance at the sign-board. He started across the slide as the prow of the *Sky-rocket*, with Nan clinging to the wheel, shot into view.

The girls shrieked in chorus—all but Nan herself. The stubborn, fat man, at last awakened to his danger, plunged ahead. There was a mighty collision!

The fat man dived head-first into a soft snow bank on one side of the slide; the bobsled plunged into another soft bank on the other side, and all the girls were buried, some of them over their heads, in the snow.

They were not hurt—

"Save in our dignity and our pompadours!" cried Laura Polk, the red-haired girl, coming to the surface like a whale, "to blow."

"Goodness—gracious—Agnes!" ejaculated the big girl, who was known as "Procrastination" Boggs. "What ever became of that man who got in our way?"

Nan Sherwood had already gotten out of the drift and had hauled her particular chum, Bess Harley, with her to the surface. Grace Mason and Lillie Nevins were crying a little; but Nan had assured herself at a glance that neither of the timid ones was hurt.

She now looked around, rather wildly, at Amelia Boggs' question. The fat man had utterly disappeared. Surely the bobsled, having struck him only a glancing blow, had not throw him completely off the earth!

Bess was looking up into the snowy tree-tops, and Laura Polk suggested that maybe the fat man had been only an hallucination.

"Hallucination! Your grandmother's hat!" exclaimed Amelia Boggs. "If his wasn't a solid body, there never was one!"

"What happens when an irresistible force meets an immovable object?" murmured Laura.

"Both must be destroyed," finished Bess. "But I see the tail of our bob, all right."

Just then Nan ran across the track. At the same moment a floundering figure, like a great polar bear in his winter coat, emerged from the opposite drift. The fat man, without his hat and with his face very red and wet, loomed up gigantically in the snow-pile.

"Oh! Nan Sherwood!" cried Laura. "Have you found him?"

The fat man glared at Nan malevolently. "So your name is Sherwood, it is?" he snarled. "You're the girl that was steering that abominable sled—and you steered it right into me."

"Oh, no, sir! Not intentionally!" cried the worried Nan.

"Yes, you did!" flatly contradicted the choleric fat man. "I saw you."

"Oh, Nan Sherwood!" gasped Amelia, "isn't he mean to say that?"

"Your name's Sherwood, is it?" growled the man. "I should think I'd had trouble enough with people of *that* name. Is your father Robert Sherwood, of Tillbury, Illinois?"

"Yes, sir," replied the wondering Nan.

"Ha! I might have known it," snarled the man, trying to beat the snow from his clothes. "I heard he had a girl up here at this school. The rascal!"

Professor Krenner had just reached the spot from the top of the hill. From below had hurried the crews of bobsleds number two and three. Linda Riggs, who led one of the crews, heard the angry fat man speaking so unfavorably of Nan Sherwood's father. She sidled over to his side of the track to catch all that he said.

Nan, amazed and hurt by the fat man's words and manner, would have withdrawn silently, had it not been for the last phrase the man used in reference to her father. Nan was very loyal, and to hear him called "rascal" was more than she could tamely hear.

"I do not know what you mean, sir," she said earnestly. "But if you really *know* my father, you know that what you say of him is wrong. He is not a rascal."

"I say he is!" ejaculated the man with the grouch.

Here Professor Krenner interfered, and he spoke quite sharply.

"You've said enough, Bulson. Are you hurt?"

"I don't know," grumbled the fat man.

"He can't tell till he's seen his lawyer," whispered Laura Polk, beginning to giggle.

"Are any of you girls hurt?" queried the professor, his red and white cap awry.

"I don't think so, Professor," Bess replied. "Only Nan's feelings. That man ought to be ashamed of himself for speaking so of Mr. Sherwood."

"Oh, I know what I'm talking about!" cried the fat man, blusteringly.

"Then you can tell it all to me, Ravell Bulson," bruskly interposed the professor again. "Come along to my cabin and I'll fix you up. Mrs. Gleason has arrived at the top of the hill and she will take charge of you young ladies. I am glad none of you is hurt."

The overturned crew hauled their bobsled out of the drift. Linda Riggs went on with her friends, dragging the *Gay Girl*.

"I'd like to hear what that fat man has to say about Sherwood's father," the ill-natured girl murmured to Cora Courtney, her roommate. "I wager he isn't any better than he ought to be."

"You don't *know*," said Cora.

"I'd like to find out. You know, I never have liked that Nan Sherwood. She is a common little thing. And I don't believe they came honestly by that money they brought from Scotland."

"Oh, Linda!" gasped Cora.

"Well, I don't!" declared the stubborn girl. "There is a mystery about the Sherwoods being rich, at all. I know they were as poor as church mice in Tillbury until Nan came here to school. I found that out from a girl who used to live there."

"Not Bess Harley?"

"No, indeed! Bess wouldn't tell anything bad about Nan. I believe she is afraid of Nan. But this girl I mean wrote me all about the Sherwoods."

"Nan is dreadfully close-mouthed," agreed Cora, who was a weak girl and quite under Linda's influence.

"Well! Those Sherwoods were never anything in Tillbury. How Bess Harley came to take up with Nan, the goodness only knows. Her father worked in one of the mills that shut down last New Year. He was out of work a long time and then came this fortune in Scotland they claim was left Mrs. Sherwood by an old uncle, or great uncle. I guess it's nothing much to brag about."

"Bess said once it might be fifty thousand dollars," said Cora, speaking the sum unctuously. Cora was poor herself and she loved money.

"Oh, maybe!" exclaimed Linda Riggs, tossing her head. "But I guess nobody knows the rights of it. Maybe it isn't so much. You know that there were other heirs who turned up when Nan's father and mother got over to Scotland, and one while Nan thought she would have to leave school because there wasn't money enough to pay her tuition fees."

"Yes, I know all about that," admitted Cora, hurriedly. She had a vivid remembrance of the unfinished letter from Nan to her mother, which she had found and shown to Linda. Cora was not proud of that act. Nan had never been anything but kind to her and secretly Cora did not believe this ill-natured history of Nan Sherwood that Linda repeated.

Those of my readers who have read the first volume of this series, entitled "Nan Sherwood at Pine Camp, Or, The Old Lumberman's Secret," will realize just how much truth and how much fiction entered into the story of Nan's affairs related by the ill-natured Linda Riggs.

When Mr. and Mrs. Sherwood started for Scotland to make sure of the wonderful legacy willed to Nan's mother by the Laird of Emberon's steward, Nan was sent up into the Peninsula of Michigan to stay with her Uncle Henry and Aunt Kate Sherwood at a lumber camp. Her adventures there during the spring and summer were quite exciting. But the most exciting thing that had happened to Nan Sherwood was the decision on her parents' part that she should go with her chum, Bess Harley, to Lakeview Hall, a beautifully situated and popular school for girls on the shore of Lake Huron.

In "Nan Sherwood at Lakeview Hall, Or, The Mystery of the Haunted Boathouse," the second volume of the series, were narrated the incidents of Nan's first term at boarding school. She and Bess made many friends and had some rivals, as was natural, for they were very human girls, in whom no angelic quality was overdeveloped.

In Linda Riggs, daughter of the rich and influential railroad president, Nan had an especially vindictive enemy. Nan had noticed Linda's eagerness to hear all the ill-natured fat man had to say about Mr. Sherwood.

"I do wish Linda had not heard that horrid man speak so of Papa Sherwood," Nan said to Bess Harley, as they toiled up the hill again after the overturning of the *Sky-rocket*.

"Oh, what do you care about Linda?" responded Bess.

"I care very much about what people say of my father," Nan said. "And the minute I get home I'm going to find out what that Bulson meant."

CHAPTER III

AN ADVENTURE ON THE RAIL

That adventurous afternoon on Pendragon Hill was the last chance the girls of Lakeview Hall had that term for bobsledding. School closed the next day and those pupils who lived farthest away, and who went home for the holidays, started that very evening by train from Freeling.

Nan and her chum, Bess Harley, were two who hurried away from the Hall. Tillbury was a night's ride from Lakeview Hall, and the chums did not wish to lose any of their short stay at home.

It had already been planned and agreed to that Nan and Bess were to go to Chicago to visit in the Masons' home during a part of this vacation, and the two friends, who knew very little of city life, were eager indeed for the new experience.

Walter and Grace had started for Chicago that morning, and when the two Tillbury girls saw how hard it was snowing when Charley, with his 'bus on runners, drove them to the station, they wished that they had asked the privilege of Dr. Beulah Prescott, the principal, of going early, too.

"This yere's goin' to be a humdinger of a storm," prophesied Charley. "You gals'll maybe get snowed up on the train."

"Oh! What fun!" cried the thoughtless Bess.

"I hope not!" proclaimed Nan.

"I think it would be fun, Nan," urged her chum.

"Humph! How about eating?" queried the red-haired girl, Laura Polk, who would be one of the party as far as the Junction.

"Oh, there's a dining-car on this train," said May Winslow, who was to speed away to the South to spend Christmas, where there was no ice or snow, and where the darkeys celebrate the holiday with fire-crackers, as Northern people do the Fourth of July.

"That's all right about the dining-car," said Nan. "All right for you girls who are going to Chicago. But our train from the Junction has no 'eats' attached and if we get snowed up—"

"Ugh!" cried her chum. "Don't suggest such a horrid possibility. I'm going right now to buy out the lunch counter and take it along with us."

"And break your teeth on adamantine sandwiches, harder than Professor Krenner's problems in algebra?" suggested May.

The red-haired girl began to laugh. "I thought Bess never would carry a shoe-box lunch again. 'Member that one you two girls from Tillbury brought to school with you, last September?"

"Will we ever forget it?" groaned Nan.

"I don't care!" exclaimed Bess. "You can't have a bite of what I buy, Laura Polk!" and she marched away to the lunch counter and spent most of her remaining pocket money on greasy pies, decrepit sandwiches, soggy "pound-cake" and crullers that might have been used with success as car-seat springs!

The train was late in arriving at Freeling. It rumbled into the station covered with snow, its pilot showing how it had ploughed through the drifts. The girls were separated at once, for Nan's seat and her chum's were in one car, while the girls bound Chicago-ward had a section in another.

Nan and Bess would be in their berths and asleep when their car should be switched to the southern line to be picked up by the other train at the Junction. So they bade their friends good-bye at once and, after a false start or two, the heavy train blundered into the night and the storm, and Freeling was left behind.

The train did not move rapidly. A few miles out of Freeling it became stalled for a while. But a huge snow-plow came to the rescue at this point and piloted the train clear into the Junction.

The sleeping-car porter wanted to make up the girls' berths at the usual hour—nine o'clock. But Nan begged hard for more time and Bess treated him to a generous lunch from the supply she had bought at Freeling. Afterwards she admitted she was sorry she was so reckless with the commissary.

Just now, however, neither Bess nor Nan worried about supplies for what Laura Polk called "the inner girl." Through the window they saw the drifts piling up along the right of way, wherever the lamps revealed them; country stations darkened and almost buried under the white mantle; and the steadily driving snow itself that slanted earthward—a curtain that shut out of sight all objects a few yards beyond the car windows.

"My! this is dreadful," murmured Bess, when the train halted again for the drifts to be shoveled out of a cot. "When do you s'pose we'll ever get home?"

"Not at eight o'clock in the morning," Nan announced promptly. "That's sure. I don't know just how many miles it is—and I never could tell anything about one of these railroad time-tables."

"Laura says she can read a menu card in a French restaurant more easily," chuckled Bess. "I wonder how their train is getting on?"

"I'm so selfishly worried about our own train that I'm not thinking of them," admitted Nan. "There! we've started again."

But the train puffed on for only a short distance and then "snubbed" its nose into another snow-bank. The wheels of the locomotive clogged, the flues filled with snow, the wet fuel all but extinguished the fire. Before the engineer could back the heavy train, the snow swirled in behind it and built a drift over the platform of the rear coach. The train was completely stalled.

This happened after eleven o'clock and while they were between stations. It was a lonely and rugged country, and even farm-houses were far apart. The train was about midway between stations, the distance from one to the other being some twenty miles. The weight of the snow had already broken down long stretches of telegraph and telephone wires. No aid for the snow-bound train and passengers could be obtained.

Before this, however, the porter had insisted upon making up the girls' berths and, like most of the other passengers in the Pullman, Nan and Bess were asleep. While the passengers slept the snow continued to sift down, building the drifts higher and higher, and causing the train-crew increasing worriment of mind.

The locomotive could no longer pierce the drifts. The train had been too heavy for her from the first. Fuel supply had been renewed at the Junction, as well as water; but the coal was now needed to keep up steam for the cars—and it would not last long for that purpose.

If the storm continued until morning without change, it might be several days before the road could be opened from either end of the division. Food and fuel would be very hard to obtain in this waste of snow, and so far from human habitation.

The two conductors and the engineer spent most of the night discussing ways and means. Meanwhile the snow continued to fall and the passengers, for the most part, rested in ignorance of the peril that threatened.

CHAPTER IV

CAST AWAY IN THE SNOW

It was Bess who came back from the ladies' room on the Pullman and startled Nan Sherwood by shaking her by the shoulder as she lay in the upper berth, demanding:

"Have you any idea what time it is, Nan? Say! have you?"

"No-o—ouch!" yawned her chum. "Goodness! That was my elbow. There's not much room on these shelves, is there?"

"Do you hear me?" shrilled Bess. "What time do you suppose it is?"

"Oh, dear me! Is that a conundrum?" asked Nan, with but faint interest.

"Wake up!" and Bess pinched her. "I never knew you so stupid before. See my watch, Nan," and she held the small gold time-piece she had owned since her last birthday, so that her chum could see its face.

"A quarter to eight," read Nan from the dial. "Well! that's not so late. I know we're allowed to remain in the car till eight. I'll hurry. But, oh! isn't it dark outside?"

"Now, you're showing a little common sense," snapped Bess. "But do you see that my watch has stopped?"

"Oh! so it has," agreed Nan. "But, then, honey, you're always letting it run down."

"I know," said Bess, impatiently. "And at first I thought it must have stopped last evening at a quarter to eight. When I woke up just now it was just as dark as it was yesterday morning at six. But I took a peep at the porter's clock and what do you think?"

"I'll shave you for nothing and give you a drink," laughed Nan, quoting the old catch-line.

Bess was too excited to notice her chum's fun. She said, dramatically:

"The porter's clock says half-past nine and half the berths are put up again at the other end of the car!"

"Mercy!" gasped Nan, and swung her feet over the edge of the berth. "Oh!" she squealed the next moment.

"What's the matter now?" demanded her chum.

"Oh! I feel like a poor soldier who's having his legs cut off. My! isn't the edge of this berth sharp?"

"But what do you know about its being half-past nine?" demanded Bess.

"And the train is standing still," said Nan. "Do you suppose we can be at Tillbury?"

"Goodness! we ought to be," said Bess. "But it is so dark."

"And Papa Sherwood would be down in the yards looking for me before this time, I know."

"Well! what do you think it means?" demanded her chum. "And b-r-r-r! it's cold. There isn't half enough steam on in this car."

Nan was scrambling into her outer garments. "I'll see about this in a minute, Bess," she said, chuckling. "Maybe the sun's forgotten to rise."

Bess had managed to draw aside the curtain of the big window. She uttered a muffled scream.

"Oh, Nan! It's sno-ow!"

"What? Still snowing?" asked her chum.

"No. It's all banked up against the pane. I can't see out at all."

"Goodness—gracious—me!" ejaculated Nan. "Do you suppose we're snowed in?"

That was just exactly what it meant. The porter, his eyes rolling, told them all about it. The train had stood just here, "in the middle of a snow-bank," since midnight. It was still snowing. And the train was covered in completely with the soft and clinging mantle.

At first the two chums bound for Tillbury were only excited and pleased by the novel situation. The porter arranged their seats for them and Bess proudly produced the box of lunch she had bought at Freeling, and of which they had eaten very little.

"Tell me how smart I am, Nan Sherwood!" she cried. "Wish we had a cup of coffee apiece."

At that very moment the porter and conductor entered the car with a steaming can of the very comforting fluid Bess had just mentioned. The porter distributed waxed paper cups from the water cooler for each passenger's use and the conductor judiciously poured the cups half full of coffee.

"You two girls are very lucky," he said, when he saw what was in the lunch-box. "Take care of your food supply. No knowing when we'll get out of this drift."

"Why, mercy!" ejaculated Bess. "I don't know that I care to live for long on stale sandwiches and pie, washed down by the most miserable coffee I ever tasted."

"Well, I suppose it's better to live on this sort of food than to die on no food at all," Nan said, laughing.

It seemed to be all a joke at first. There were only a few people in the Pullman, and everybody was cheerful and inclined to take the matter pleasantly. Being snow-bound in a train was such a novel experience that no unhappy phase of the situation deeply impressed any of the passengers' minds.

Breakfast was meagre, it was true. The "candy butcher," who sold popcorn and sandwiches as well, was bought out at an exorbitant price by two traveling men, who distributed what they had secured with liberal hand. Bess, more cautious than usual, hid the remains of her lunch and told Nan that it was "buried treasure."

"Castaways ought to find treasure buried on their island to make it really interesting," she told her chum. "Think of poor Robinson Crusoe and his man Friday. Wouldn't they have been just tickled to death to have found anything like this for their Sunday dinner, say?"

"I don't believe Friday would have cared much about railroad lunch apple pies," said Nan. "One's palate has to become accustomed to such delicacies."

"Now, don't be critical, Nan Sherwood, or I sha'n't give you any more pie," cried Bess. "B-r-r-r! isn't it cold in here?"

"We really ought to speak to the janitor about it," said Nan, demurely. "He isn't giving us enough steam. I shall move into another apartment before next winter if they can't heat this one any better."

They whiled away the morning in conversation and reading. They had to sit with their furs on. Nan looked like a little Esquimaux in hers, for her Uncle Henry Sherwood had bought them for her to wear in the Big Woods the winter before. Finally Bess declared she was too fidgety to sit still any longer.

"I've just got to do something. Here's the conductor again. Let's stir him up about the heat."

"I wouldn't," said more thoughtful Nan. "He looks as though he had his own troubles."

"I don't care! We can't sit here and freeze to death. Say, Mr. Conductor, can't we have any more heat? We're really almost frozen."

"Can't help it, little ladies," responded the man, rather gruffly. "You'll find it worse when the coal gives out entirely."

"Oh, mercy!" Bess exclaimed, when he had gone on. "What a bear!"

But Nan looked suddenly disturbed. "Do you suppose that is possible?" she asked.

"What's possible?"

"That the coal may give out?"

"What if it does?" queried her chum, blankly.

"Goodness me! How will they make steam if there's no fuel for the fire?"

"Oh!" gasped Bess, "I never thought of that. Goodness, Nan, we'll be frozen to icicles!"

"Not yet, I hope," said Nan, getting up briskly. "Let's see if we can't stick our heads out of doors. I'm aching for a breath of fresh air."

They went forward and opened the vestibule door. The outside doors were locked and the snow was piled against the little windows, high up in the door panels.

"I believe this snow is piled completely over the cars," declared Nan.

"Isn't that funny?" said Bess. "How do you s'pose they'll ever dig us out?"

"I wonder if it has stopped snowing?"

"I hope so!"

"We can't hear anything down here," continued Nan. "But we naturally couldn't, if the train is buried in the snow."

"Dear me, Nan!" said her chum, in a really worried tone. "What do you s'pose will happen to us?"

"We—ell—"

"And our folks! They'll be awfully worried. Why! we should have been at Tillbury by eight o'clock, and here it is noon!"

"That is so," Nan said, with more assurance. "But of course they know what has happened to the train. We're in no real danger."

"We—ell, I s'pose not," admitted Bess, slowly. "But it does seem funny."

Nan chuckled. "As long as we see anything funny in the situation, I guess we shall get along all right."

"Oh! you know what I mean," her chum said. "I wonder where that door leads to?"

"Into another car," Nan said demurely.

"Is that so, Miss Smartie?" cried Bess. "But what car?"

She tried the door. It gave entrance to a baggage coach, dimly lit by a lantern swinging from the roof. Nobody was in the car and the girls walked hesitatingly forward.

"Oh!" squealed Bess, suddenly. "Here's my trunk."

"And here's mine," Nan said, and stopped to pat the side of the battered, brown box stenciled "N.S." on its end. Nan had something very precious in that trunk, and to tell the truth she wished she had that precious possession out of the trunk right then.

"It's awfully cold in here, Bess," she said slowly.

"I guess they haven't got the steam turned on in this flat, either," returned Bess, laughing. "Nothing to freeze here but the trunks. Oh! oh! what's that?"

Her startled cry was caused by a sudden sound from a dark corner — a whimpering cry that might have been a baby's.

"The poor thing!" cried Nan, darting toward the sound. "They have forgotten it, I know."

"A baby in a baggage car?" gasped Bess. "Whoever heard the like?"

CHAPTER V

WAIFS AND STRAYS

"What a cruel, cruel thing!" Nan murmured.

"I never supposed the railroad took babies as baggage," said her chum wonderingly.

At that Nan uttered a laugh that was half a sob. "Silly! reach down that lantern, please. Stand on the box. I'll show you what sort of a baby it is."

Bess obeyed her injunction and brought the light. Nan was kneeling in the corner before a small crate of slats in which was a beautiful, brown-eyed, silky haired water spaniel—nothing but a puppy—that was licking her hands through his prison bars and wriggling his little body as best he could in the narrow quarters to show his affection and delight.

"Well, I never!" cried Bess, falling on her knees before the dog's carrier, and likewise worshipping. "Isn't he the cunning, tootsie-wootsie sing? 'E 'ittle dear! Oh, Nan! isn't he a love? How soft his tiny tongue is," for the puppy was indiscriminate in his expressions of affection.

"I believe the men must have forgotten him," said Nan.

"It's a murderin' shame, as cook would say," Bess declared. "Let's let him out."

"Oh, no! we mustn't—not till we've asked leave."

"Well, who'll we ask?" demanded Bess.

"The baggage-man, of course," said Nan, jumping up. "I believe he's hungry, too."

"Who? the baggage-man?" giggled Bess.

"The puppy, of course," returned Nan.

"We'll feed him some of our pie," suggested Bess.

"He ought to have some warm milk," Nan said seriously.

"Oh, indeed!" exclaimed her chum. "Well, Nan Sherwood, I don't think anybody's thought to milk the cow this morning."

"Oh, be good, Bess," Nan admonished her. The pup began to whimper again. "Come on; let's find the man."

The girls ventured farther forward. When they opened the door of the car at that end, Bess screamed outright.

"Why! it's a tunnel, Nan," she ejaculated. "Do you see?"

"What a lot of snow there must be above us," her chum rejoined, with gravity.

"Why, this is just the greatest adventure that ever happened," Bess continued. "The men have tunneled through the drift from one car to the other. I wonder how thick the roof is, Nan? Suppose it falls on us!"

"Not likely," responded her chum, and she stepped confidently out upon the platform. The door of the forward car stuck and after a moment somebody came and slid it back a crack.

"Hullo, young ladies!" exclaimed the brakeman, who looked out. "What do you want forward, here?"

"We want to speak to the baggage-man, please," Nan said promptly.

"Hey, Jim!" shouted the brakeman. "Here's a couple of ladies to see you. I bet they've got something to eat in their trunks and want to open them."

There was a laugh in chorus from the crew in the forward baggage and express car. Then an older man came and asked the girls what they wished. Bess had grown suddenly bashful, so it was Nan who asked about the dog.

"The poor little thing should be released from that crate," she told the man. "And I believe he's hungry."

"I reckon you're right, Miss," said the baggage-man. "I gave him part of my coffee this morning; but I reckon that's not very satisfying to a dog."

"He should have some milk," Nan announced decidedly.

"Ya—as?" drawled the baggage-man. He had come into the car with the girls and now looked down at the fretting puppy. "Ya—as," he repeated; "but where are you going to get milk?"

"From the so-called cow-tree," said Bess soberly, "which is found quite commonly in the jungles of Brazil. You score the bark and the wood immediately beneath it with an axe, or machette, insert a sliver of clean wood, and the milky sap trickles forth into your cup—"

"How ridiculous!" interposed Nan, while the baggage-man burst into appreciative laughter.

"Well," said Bess, "when folks are cast away like us, don't they always find the most wonderful things all about them—right to their hands, as it were?"

"Like a cow-tree in a baggage car?" said Nan, with disgust.

"Well! how do *you* propose to find milk here?" demanded her chum.

"Why," said Nan, with assurance, "I'd look through the express matter and see if there wasn't a case of canned milk going somewhere—"

"Great! Hurrah for our Nan!" broke in Bess Harley, in admiration. "Who'd ever have thought of that?"

"But we couldn't do that, Miss," said the baggage-man, scratching his head. "We'd get into trouble with the company."

"So the poor dog must starve," said Bess, saucily.

"Guess he'll have to take his chance with the rest of us," said the man.

"Oh! You don't mean we're all in danger of starvation?" gasped Bess, upon whose mind this possibility had not dawned before.

"Well—" said the man, and then stopped.

"They'll come and dig us out, won't they?" demanded Bess.

"Oh, yes."

"Then we won't starve," she said, with satisfaction.

But Nan did not comment upon this at all. She only said, with confidence:

"Of course you can let this poor doggy out of the cage and we will be good to him."

"Well, Miss, that altogether depends upon the conductor, you know. It's against the rules for a dog to be taken into a passenger coach."

"I do think," cried Bess, "that this is the very meanest railroad that ever was. I am sure that Linda Riggs' father owns it. To keep a poor, dear, little dog like that, freezing and starving, in an old baggage car."

"Do you know President Riggs, Miss?" interrupted the baggage-man.

"Why—" began Bess, but her chum interposed before she could go further.

"We know Mr. Riggs' daughter very well. She goes to school where we do, at Lakeview Hall. She was on this train till it was split at the Junction, last evening."

"Well, indeed, Miss, you tell that to Mr. Carter. If you are friends of Mr. Riggs' daughter, maybe he'll stretch a point and let you take the dog into the Pullman. I don't suppose anybody will object at a time like this."

"How could you, Nan?" demanded Bess, in a whisper. "Playing up Linda Riggs' name for a favor?"

"Not for ourselves, no, indeed!" returned Nan, in the same low tone. "But for the poor doggy, yes."

"Say! I wonder what she'd say if she knew?"

"Something mean, of course," replied Nan, calmly. "But we'll save that poor dog if we can. Come on and find this Conductor Carter."

They left the puppy yelping after them as they returned to the Pullman. The cars felt colder now and the girls heard many complaints as they walked through to the rear. The conductor, the porter said, had gone back into the smoking car. That car was between the Pullman and the day coaches.

When Nan rather timidly opened the door of the smoking car a burst of sound rushed out, almost startling in its volume—piercing cries of children, shrill tones of women's voices, the guttural scolding of men, the expostulations of the conductor himself, who had a group of complainants about him, and the thunderous snoring of a fat man in the nearest seat, who slept with his feet cocked up on another seat and a handkerchief over his face.

"Goodness!" gasped Bess, pulling back. "Let's not go in. It's a bear garden."

"Why, I don't understand it," murmured Nan. "Women and children in the smoker? Whoever heard the like?"

"They've turned off the heat in the other two cars and made us all come in here, lady," explained a little dark-haired and dark-eyed woman who sat in a seat near the door. "They tell us there is not much coal, and they cannot heat so many cars."

She spoke without complaint, in the tone of resignation so common among the peasantry of Europe, but heard in North America from but two people—the French Canadian and the peon of Mexico. Nan had seen so many of the former people in the Big Woods of Upper Michigan the summer before, that she was sure this poor woman was a "Canuck." Upon her lap lay a delicate, whimpering, little boy of about two years.

"What is the matter with the poor little fellow, madam?" asked Nan, compassionately.

"With my little Pierre, mademoiselle?" returned the woman.

"Yes," said Nan.

"He cries for food, mademoiselle," said the woman simply. "He has eaten nothing since we left the Grand Gap yesterday at three o'clock; except that the good conductor gave us a drink of coffee this morning. And his mother has nothing to give her poor Pierre to eat. It is sad, is it not?"

CHAPTER VI

A SERIOUS PROBLEM

The chums from Tillbury looked at each other in awed amazement. Nothing just like this had ever come to their knowledge before. The healthy desire of a vigorous appetite for food was one thing; but this child's whimpering need and its mother's patient endurance of her own lack of food for nearly twenty-four hours, shook the two girls greatly.

"Why, the poor little fellow!" gasped Nan, and sank to her knees to place her cheek against the pale one of the little French boy.

"They—they're starving!" choked Bess Harley.

The woman seemed astonished by the emotion displayed by these two schoolgirls. She looked from Nan to Bess in rather a frightened way.

"Monsieur, the conductor, say it cannot ver' well be help'," she murmured. "It is the snow; it haf overtaken us."

"It just *can* be helped!" cried Bess, suddenly, and she whirled and fairly ran forward into the chair car. Nan did not notice her chum's departure at the moment. The baby had seized her finger and was smiling at her. Such a pretty little fellow, but so weak and ill in appearance.

"Oh, madame!" Nan cried in her best French, "is it not terrible? We may be here for hours."

"As the good God wills," said the woman, patiently. "We cannot devise or shape Fate, mademoiselle."

Nan stood up and shook her head, saying vigorously, and in her own tongue, for she was too much moved to remember Mademoiselle Loro's teaching:

"But we need not accept Fate's determination as final, I am sure! There is a good God, as you say, madam. This child must have food, and—"

At the moment Bess rushed in carrying the paste-board box containing the remains of their lunch. "Here!" she cried, dramatically. "Give the poor little fellow this."

"Oh, little ladies!" responded the woman, "have a care. You will have need of this food yourselves."

"No, no!" cried Bess, the impetuous. "We are stuffed to repletion. Aren't we, Nan?"

"We have certainly eaten much more recently than madam and the little one," agreed Nan, heartily.

The woman opened the box. The child sat up with a crow of delight. The mother gave him one of the stale crullers, and he began gnawing on it with all the gusto of a hungry dog on a bone.

"Take something yourself, madam," commanded Nan. "And more for the little fellow."

"Let 'em have it all, Nan," whispered the impulsive Bess. "Goodness! we can get on somehow."

But Nan was more observant than her chum. There were other children in the car besides this little fellow. In fact, in the seat but one behind the French woman and her baby, a girl of six or seven years was clinging to the seat-back and staring with hungry eyes at the broken food in the box.

"Gracious!" gasped Bess, seeing this little one when Nan had nudged her and pointed. "Gracious! that's the picture of Famine, herself."

She seized one of the greasy little pies and thrust it into the child's hands. The latter began devouring it eagerly. Bess saw other hungry mouths open and eager hands outstretched.

"Oh, Nan!" she almost sobbed. "We've got to give them all some. All the poor little children!"

Her chum did not try to curb Bess Harley's generosity. There was not much of the food left, so there was no danger of over-feeding any of the small children who shared in the generosity of the chums. But when the last crumb was gone they found the conductor at their elbows.

"Well, girls!" he exclaimed grimly. "Now you've done it, haven't you?"

"Done what, sir?" asked Bess, rather startled.

"You've given away all your own lunch. What did I tell you? I warned you to take care of it."

"Oh, sir!" cried Nan. "We couldn't have eaten it, knowing that these little folks were so hungry."

"No, indeed!" agreed Bess.

"If you had remained in your own car," the conductor said, "you would have known nothing about these poor kiddies."

"Well, I'm glad we did find out about 'em before we ate our lunch all up," declared Nan.

"Why, I'd like to know, Miss?" asked the man.

"It would have lain heavily on our consciences—"

"And surely injured our digestions," giggled Bess. "That pie was something awful."

"Well, it's all gone now, and you have nothing."

"Oh, that's not the worst," cried Bess, suddenly. "Oh, Nan!" and she clasped her gloved hands tragically.

"What is it now?" asked her chum.

"The poor little dog! He won't have even railroad pie to eat."

"What dog is this?" demanded the conductor.

"Oh!" cried Nan. "Are you Mr. Carter?"

"Yes, I am, Miss. But this dog?"

"Is in the baggage car," Nan said eagerly. "And he's so cold and hungry and lonesome. He's just crying his heart out."

"He is?"

"Won't you let us take him into our car where it is warmer and take care of him?"

"That nuisance of a pup?" demanded the conductor, yet with twinkling eyes that belied his gruffness. "I know he's yapping his little head off."

"Then let us have him, sir, do!" begged Nan earnestly.

"Take him into the Pullman, you mean?"

"Yes, sir, we'll take the best care of him," promised Nan.

"Against the rules!" declared the conductor, briskly.

"But rules ought to be broken at times," urged Nan. "For instance, can't they be relaxed when folks are cast away on desert islands?"

"Oh, ho!" chuckled the conductor. "I see the point, Miss. But the captain of the ship must maintain discipline, just the same, on the desert island as aboard ship."

"I s'pose you've got to enforce the rule against passengers riding on the platform, too, even if we are stuck in a snowdrift?" Bess said a little crossly. They had come out into the vestibule, and she was cold.

The conductor broke into open laughter at this; but Nan was serious.

"Suppose anything happens to the poor little fellow?" she fumed. "He may get cold. And he certainly will starve."

"Have you anything more in the line of food to give away?" demanded the conductor.

"Not a crumb," sighed Bess. "By the time the cannibals arrive at this desert island we'll all be too thin to tempt them to a banquet."

"But there may be something on the train with which to feed that poor doggie," insisted Nan.

"If you mean in the crew's kettles," said the conductor, "I can assure you, young lady, there is nothing. This crew usually eats at the end of the division. It's not like a freight train crew. We'd be a whole lot better off right now," added the conductor, reflectively, "if we had a caboose attached to the end of this train. We'd stand a chance of rustling up some grub for all these hungry people."

"Oh, dear!" gasped Bess. "Do you s'pose we're going to be hungry long?"

"They say one doesn't notice it much after about eight days," her chum said, chuckling.

"Ugh!" shivered Bess, "I don't much care for your kind of humor, Nan Sherwood."

The conductor suddenly glanced at Nan more keenly and asked, "Are you Nancy Sherwood, Miss?"

"Why, yes, sir."

"And you go to school somewhere upon the shore of Lake Huron?" he pursued.

"Why, yes, sir."

"We go to Lakeview Hall. And we know Linda Riggs," blurted out Bess, remembering what the baggage-man had advised them to say to the conductor.

"Oh, indeed?" said Mr. Carter; but his interest remained fixed on Nan. "You didn't go to school last September over this division, did you?" he asked.

"No, sir. We went from Chicago," replied the wondering Nan.

"Your train was broke in two at the Junction to put in a car?"

"Yes, sir."

"And what did you do at the Junction?" asked the conductor, quickly.

"Oh, I know!" cried Bess, as her chum hesitated. "She got off the train and killed a big rattlesnake that was just going to bite a little girl—yes, you did, Nan Sherwood!"

"You're the girl, Miss!" declared Mr. Carter, drawing out his notebook and pencil. "There have been some inquiries made for you."

"Mercy!" ejaculated Nan. "I don't want to hear anything more about that old snake."

The conductor laughed. "I fancy you won't hear anything unpleasant about the snake," he said. "Where do you live, Nancy Sherwood?"

"I live at Tillbury," Nan said. "But I sha'n't be home much this vacation."

"Where will you be, then, about the first of the year?"

"I'll tell you," Bess cried briskly, and she gave Mr. Carter Mr. Mason's address in Chicago.

The conductor wrote it down carefully in his notebook. Nan was impatient.

"Can't you find something among the express packages to help us out, sir?" she asked. "Canned goods. For instance, a case of canned milk?"

"We'll see, Miss," said the conductor, starting forward again. "At any rate, I'll let you two girls have the dog."

CHAPTER VII

THE FAT MAN INTERPOSES

The people in the Pullman car, who were much more comfortably situated than those in the smoking car, or than the crew of the train hived up in the first baggage coach, were beginning to complain a good deal now. The colored porter, with rolling eyes and appealing gestures, met the conductor and the two girls.

"Ah kyan't stan' this no longer, Mistah Ca'tah," he almost sobbed. "Da's sumpin' got t' be did fo' all dese starbin white ladies an' gemmen—ya-as sah! Dey is jes' about drivin' me mad. I kyan't stan' it."

"What can't you stand, Nicodemus?" demanded Mr. Carter, good-naturedly.

"Dey is a-groanin' an' a-takin' on powerful bad 'cause dey ain't no dining kyar cotched up wid us yet."

"Dining car caught up with us?" gasped Nan and Bess together.

"What sort of a yarn have you been giving these passengers, Nick?" demanded the conductor.

"Well, Ah jes' done got t' tell 'em sumpin' t' pacify 'em," whispered the darkey. "No use lettin' 'em think dey gwyne t' starb t' death. Ah tell 'em yo' done sent back t' de Junction for a car-load ob eats an' dat it's expected t' arrive any hour. Ya-as, sah!"

"Why, you atrocious falsifier!" ejaculated Mr. Carter.

"Wot! me?" exclaimed the porter. "No, sah! Ah ain't nottin' like dat—no, sah! Ah reckon Ah done save dat little man's life. Yo' know, dat little drummer wot's trabelin' wid de big man. Dey was castin' lots t' see which one should be kilt fo' to be et by de odder—"

"Oh, mercy!" screamed Bess, and stuffed her handkerchief into her mouth.

"Ya-as, indeedy, Miss! Dey was gettin' mighty desprit. An de big feller, he says, 'Hit don't much matter which way de dice falls, I'm de bigges' an' I certainly kin holt ma own wid a little runt like you!' He says jes' lak' dat to his friend, de littles' feller."

Nan and Bess both hid their faces behind Mr. Carter's broad back.

"Ah got nervous," pursued the darkey. "Dat big man looked lak' he was jes' going t' start right in on his fren'. An' de luck turns his way, anyhow, and de lil' feller loses. 'I gibs yo' 'twill six-thirty to-night,' de big man says. 'Dat's ma reg'lar dinner hour, an' I'm moughty savage ef I go much over ma dinner time.'

"Golly, boss!" added the porter, "Ah jes' 'bleeged tun say sumpin', an Ah tells 'em de dinin' kyar'll sho'ly obertake us fo' six-thirty. Ya'as, indeedy. An' den, dar's dat lady up dar wid de sour-vinegary sort o' face. Ah jes' heard her say she'd be fo'ced tuh eat her back-comb if she didn't have her lunch pu'ty soon. A' yo' knows, Mistah Ca'tah, no lady's indigestion is a-gwine tuh stan' up under no sech fodder as dat."

"You old silly!" ejaculated the conductor. "These people have been fooling you. I'll separate those two drummers so that they won't eat each other—or concoct any more stories with which to worry you, Nick. Come on, young ladies. We'll see about that dog."

"And look through the express matter—do!" begged Nan.

"Surely will," replied the conductor. "But I expect we'll have to tie and muzzle the express messenger."

Bess thought this funny, too, and she giggled again. In fact, Nan declared her chum had a bad case of the "giggles" and begged her to behave herself.

"I don't believe that castaways set out to explore their island for food in any such light-minded manner as you display, Elizabeth," Nan observed.

"Oh, dear! I can't help it," Bess gasped. "That darkey is so funny. He's just as innocent as—as—"

"The man, Friday," finished Nan.

"Goody! that's who he is," agreed Bess. "He's Friday. Oh! if Laura Polk were only here, wouldn't she have lots of fun with him?"

"Seems as though those two drummers were bothering poor Friday quite enough."

They heard the little spaniel yelping the moment they opened the baggage car door.

"The poor 'ittle sing!" cooed Bess, running to the corner where the puppy was imprisoned. "Oh! how cold it is in here. It would be a little icicle, so it would be, in a little while."

"Let's see where he's going, and whom he belongs to," Mr. Carter said. "I'll have to make a note of this, and so will Jim, the baggage-man. You want to take good care of this little tyke, for the railroad is responsible for him while he is in transit."

He stooped down and brought his light to bear upon the tag wired to the top of the crate. "Ravell Bulson, Jr., Owneyville, Illinois," he read aloud, making a note of it in his book.

"Oh!" ejaculated Nan.

"Oh!" repeated Bess.

Then both together the chums gasped: "That fat man!"

"Hullo!" observed the conductor, slipping the toggles out of the hasp, which kept the door of the dog crate closed. "Do you girls know the owner of this pup? You seem to know everybody."

"We know a Mr. Ravell Bulson by sight, Mr. Carter," Nan said quietly.

"And he's just the meanest man!" began impulsive Bess; but her chum stopped her with a glance.

"Well! Mr. Ravell Bulson, Jr., has a fine pup here," declared the conductor, releasing the agitated little creature.

The spaniel could not show his delight sufficiently when he was out of the crate. He capered about them, licking the girl's shoes, tumbling down in his haste and weakness, and uttering his funny little bark in excited staccato.

Bess finally grabbed him up and, after kissing her, suddenly, right under the ear, and making her squeal, he snuggled down in her arms, his little pink tongue hanging out and his eyes shining (so Bess declared) like "two brown stars."

"'Brown stars' is good," chuckled Nan. "You'll be talking about a cerise sky next, with a pea-green sun."

"Such a carping critic!" returned Bess. "But what care I? His eyes are brown stars, so now! And if you're not very good, Nan Sherwood, I'll make him bite you."

Mr. Carter was leading the way to the forward car, and the girls followed with the spaniel. It seemed a little lighter under the tunneled snow-bank between the two cars, and the conductor said, with some satisfaction:

"I believe it has stopped snowing and will clear up. I do surely hope that is the weather programme. We want to get out of here."

"And walk to Tillbury?" cried Nan.

"It would be one good, long walk," responded the conductor, grimly. "Hi, Jim!" he added to the baggage-man, whose face appeared through the tobacco smoke that filled the forward baggage car. "Jim, these young ladies are going to take care of the pup. Belongs to Ravell Bulson, Jr., Owneyville, Illinois. Make a note of it."

"Sure!" Jim said.

"Say! that's a funny thing," put in another man, who wore the lettered cap of the express company. "I've been looking over my way-bill, Carter, and a man named Ravell Bulson of that same address has shipped a package to himself from the Bancroft Creamery siding, up above Freeling. Package marked 'Glass—handle with care.'"

"Bully!" exclaimed the conductor. "That's condensed milk in glass jars, I bet. A number-one product. I've seen it. Anything else eatable on your list?"

"Not a thing, Carter."

"How far will twenty-four cans of condensed milk go among this gang of starving people?" growled a man in overalls and a greasy cap, whom the girls knew must be the engineer.

"You keep the fire up, Horace, so's we can melt snow," said the conductor, "and we can dilute the milk all right. It's good stuff."

"Fire!" exclaimed the engineer. "How do you expect my fireman to keep up a blaze under that boiler on the shag-end of nothing? I tell you the fire's going out in less than an hour. She ain't making a pound of steam right now."

"Great Peter, Horace!" ejaculated Mr. Carter, "don't say that. We have *got* to have fire!"

"Well, you show me how to keep one going," said the engineer. "Unless you know some way of burning snow, I don't see how you're going to do it."

"Take it from me, we must find a way to keep steam up in these cars," said Mr. Carter. "We've shut off the last two cars. The smoker's packed with passengers as tight as a can of sardines."

"Oh! I wish he wouldn't talk about things eatable," groaned Bess, in Nan's ear.

"Better put the women and the children in the Pullman," suggested the baggage-man.

"Can't. Their tickets don't call for first-class accommodations," said the conductor, stubbornly, "and none of them wants to pay the difference in tariff."

"You've got your hands full, Carter," said the express messenger. "How about the case of milk?" and he dragged a box into the middle of the floor.

"Say! you fellows let that case alone," exclaimed an unpleasant voice. "That's mine. You the conductor? I have been hunting all over for you."

Nan and Bess had both turned, startled, when this speech began. It came from the fat man whom they had seen asleep in the smoking car. And, now that his face was revealed, the chums recognized Mr. Ravell Bulson, the man who had spoken so harshly of Nan's father the day of the collision on Pendragon Hill.

"Say! this is the expressman, I guess," pursued Mr. Bulson. "You're the man I really want to see. You'll see my name on that box—'R. Bulson, Owneyville, Illinois.' That's me. And I want to open that box and get something out of it."

CHAPTER VIII

SI SNUBBINS DROPS IN

"Do let's get out of here before he sees us," whispered Nan to her chum.

"No, I won't," returned Bess, in the same tone. "I want to hear how it comes out."

"Of course that horrid man won't let them use the milk for the poor little children on the train. And, goodness, Bess! you've got his dog right in your arms this moment."

"Well," said the stubborn Bess, "if that fat man takes a jar of condensed milk out of that box for himself, I'll make him give this poor little puppy some of it. Now you see if I don't!"

At first it did not look as though the fat man was going to get any of the milk even for his own consumption. The expressman said gruffly: "I can't let you open the package. It's against the rules of the company."

"Say! I shipped this package to myself. Here's the receipt," blustered Mr. Bulson. "I guess I can withdraw it from your care if I like."

"Guess again, mister," returned the expressman. "You've got three guesses, anyway."

The fat man was so assertive and over-bearing that it amused the chums from Tillbury to hear him thus flouted.

"I guess you don't know who I am?" cried the choleric fat man.

"You say your name is Bullhead—"

"Bulson!" roared the other. "Ravell Bulson. I own that milk."

"So it is condensed milk in that box, Mr. Bulson?" here interposed Mr. Carter, the conductor.

"Yes, it is," said Bulson, shortly. "I had business up near the Bancroft Creamery, and I stepped in there and bought a case of milk in glass, and shipped it home. I saw it being put aboard the express car of the other train and I had an idea it would be transferred at the Junction to this train. And here it is, and I want it."

"You're a public spirited citizen, Mr. Bulson," the conductor said suavely. "I expect you want to get this milk to divide among your fellow passengers? Especially among the children on the train?"

"What's that?" exclaimed Bulson, his eyes fairly bulging out with surprise.

"You are going to open the case of canned milk for the benefit of all hands?" said Mr. Carter, sternly.

"Wha—what do you take me for?" blurted out the fat man, indignantly. "Why, that's my milk! I'm not going to give it to anybody. What do you take me for?" he repeated.

The disgust and indignation with which Mr. Carter eyed him must have plainly shown a less thick-skinned mortal just what the conductor's opinion was. But Mr. Ravell Bulson, like most utterly selfish men, saw nothing.

"You must think I'm silly," pursued Bulson. "I shall want but a can or two for myself. Of course they'll come and plow us out before long. And I promised my wife to send that milk home."

"Wouldn't you even give any of that milk to this poor little puppy?" suddenly demanded Bess, whose anger at the fat man had been gradually rising until now, before Nan could stop her, it boiled over.

"Heh? Who are *you*, Miss, if I may inquire?" snapped the fat man.

"It doesn't matter who I am," proclaimed Bess. "I wouldn't take a drop of that milk from you, anyway. But this poor little puppy is starving."

"Why, I declare!" interrupted Bulson. "That's the little dog I shipped to Junior."

"It's your own dog, Mr. Bulson," Bess declared. "And he's almost starved."

"And what are *you* doing with him?" demanded the fat man, rage suddenly narrowing his eyes again. "What kind of actions are these?" and he swung on the members of the train crew once more. "My dog is given to any Tom, Dick, and Harry that comes along, while I can't get at my own case of milk. Preposterous!"

The express messenger had received a signal from Mr. Carter, and now said:

"I tell you what it is, Mr. Bulson; I can't help you out. The matter is entirely out of my hands. Just before you came in the conductor levied on all my goods in transit and claimed the right to seize your case of milk for the benefit of the passengers. You'll have to send in your claim to our company, and it will get the value of the milk from the railroad people for you. That's all there is to it."

"What?" roared Mr. Bulson, aghast at these words.

"You heard me," responded the expressman, handing Mr. Carter a hammer and nail puller.

The conductor kneeled down and proceeded to open the box. The fat man would have torn his hair only he was bald and there was none he could spare.

"Get away from that box! get away!" he commanded, fairly dancing about the car. "Do you know what I'll do? I'll sue the company."

"All right. Begin suit at once," growled Mr. Carter. "Get out an injunction right away. Don't fret; you'll get your share of the milk with the rest of us."

"Why, it's *all* mine," croaked the fat man, hoarse with wrath. "I'll show you—"

"Go 'way," ordered a burly brakeman, pushing him aside, and stooping to help pull off the cover of the box. "You ought to be taken out and dumped in the snow, mister. It would cool you off."

"Come, Bess!" urged Nan, anxiously. "Let's go away. We'll get the milk for the puppy afterward. I'm afraid there will be trouble."

"I wish they would throw that mean old Bulson into the snow. He deserves it," Bess returned bitterly.

"Do let's go away," Nan said again, as the men's voices became louder.

"Oh, dear me! you never will let me have any fun," declared Bess, her eyes sparkling.

"Do you call a public brawl, fun?" demanded Nan, as they opened the door of the car.

At that moment, just as the two girls with the squirming, shivering puppy, were about to step out upon the platform between the baggage cars, they were startled by a muffled shout from overhead.

"Oh! what's that?" gasped Bess.

Both she and Nan looked up. Lumps of snow from the roof of the tunnel began to fall. Then came a louder shout and a pair of booted legs burst through the roof.

"Goodness—gracious—me!" cried Nan. "Here comes—"

"An angelic visitor!" squealed Bess.

With another shout of alarm, a snow-covered figure plunged to the platform. The cowhide boots landed first, so the man remained upright. He carried a can in each hand, and all around the covers was frozen milk, betraying at once the nature of his load.

He was a slim, wiry man, in a ragged greatcoat, a cap pulled over his ears, sparkling, little, light-blue eyes of phenomenal shrewdness, and a sparse, strawcolor chin-whisker.

"Wall, I vow to Maria!" gasped the newcomer. "What's this I've dropped into?"

Bess was now laughing so that she could not speak, and the puppy was barking as hard as he could bark. Nan managed to ask:

"Who are you, sir, and where did you come from?"

"Si Snubbras is my name," declared the "heavenly visitor." "And I reckon I'm nearer home than you be, Miss, for I live right east of the railroad-cut, here. I was jest goin' across to Peleg Morton's haouse with this yere milk, when I—I sorter dropped in," and Farmer Snubbins went off into a fit of laughter at his own joke.

CHAPTER IX

AN ANGEL WITH CHIN WHISKERS

Mr. Si Snubbins was a character, and he plainly was very much pleased with himself. His little, sharp eyes apprehended the situation quickly.

"I vow to Maria!" repeated the farmer. "Ye air all snowed up here, ain't ye? A hull trainful o' folks. Wall!"

"And oh, Mr. Snubbins!" said Nan Sherwood, "you have milk in those cans, haven't you?"

"Sure have, Miss."

"Oh, Mr. Carter!" called Nan, running back into the forward car; "here's a man with *fresh* milk. You don't have to take Mr. Bulson's."

"What's that?" demanded the baggage-man, Jim, in surprise. "Where'd he get it? From that cow-tree your friend was telling us about?"

"What's this about fresh milk?" asked Mr. Carter. "Be still, Bulson. You roar to fit your name. We can't hear the little lady."

"Who's that?" snarled the excited Bulson, glaring at Nan. "How came that girl on this train? Isn't that the Sherwood girl?"

But nobody paid the fat man much attention just then. The crew crowded after Nan and Mr. Carter toward the open door of the car.

"Hul-lo" exclaimed Mr. Carter, when he saw the farmer and realized how he had "dropped in." "That milk for sale?"

"Why, mister," drawled Snubbins, "I'm under contrac' ter Peleg Morton ter deliver two cans of milk to him ev'ry day. I wasn't goin' to have him claim I hadn't tried ter fulfil my part of the contrac', so I started 'cross-lots with the cans."

"How's he going to get the milk to the creamery?" demanded Mr. Carter, shrewdly.

Si's eyes twinkled. "That's his part of the contrac'; 'tain't mine," he said. "But if ye ax me, I tell ye honest, Mr. Conductor, I don't see how

Nan Sherwood's Winter Holidays

Peleg's goin' ter do it. This is a sight the heaviest snow we've had for ten year."

"What'll you sell that milk for?" interrupted the anxious conductor. "Fresh milk will be a whole lot better for these kiddies we've got in the smoker than condensed milk. Just the same," he added, "I shall hold on to Bulson's shipment."

"What'll I take for this milk, mister?" repeated Snubbins, cautiously. "Wall, I dunno. I'spect the price has gone up some, because o' the roads being blocked."

"That will do—that will do," Mr. Carter hastened to say. "I'll take the milk, give you a receipt, and you can fight it out with the claim agent. I believe," added Mr. Carter, his lips twisting into a grim smile, "that you are the farmer whose cow was killed by this very train last fall, eh?"

"Ya-as," said Si Snubbins, sorrowfully. "Poor Sukey! She never knew what hit her."

"But the claim agent knew what hit the road when you put in your claim. That old cow wasn't worth more than ten dollars and you demanded fifty. Don't raise the tariff on this milk proportionately, for I'm sure the agent will not allow the claim."

Mr. Snubbins grinned and chuckled.

"I'll run my risk—I'll run my risk," he responded. "You kin have the milk for nawthin', if ye want it so bad. Bein' here all night, I expect ye be purty sharp-set, the whole on ye."

Mr. Carter had picked up the cans and had gone forward to have the milk thawed out at the boiler fire. Some of the brakemen had cleared away the snow by now and there was an open passage to the outside world. The keen kind blew in, and the pale, wintry sunshine lighted the space between the baggage cars. Mr. Snubbins grinned in his friendly way at the two girls.

"I reckon you gals," he said, "would just like to be over to my house where my woman could fry you a mess of flap-jacks. How's that?"

"Oh, don't mention it!" groaned Bess.

"Is your house near?" asked Nan.

"Peleg's the nighest. 'Tain't so fur. And when ye git out on top o' the snow, the top's purty hard. It blew so toward the end of that blizzard that the drifts air packed good."

"Yet you broke through," Bess said.

"Right here, I did, for a fac'" chuckled the farmer. "But it's warm down here and it made the snow soft."

"Of course!" cried Nan Sherwood. "The stale air from the cars would naturally make the roof of the tunnel soft."

"My goodness! Can't you see the train at all from up there?" Bess demanded. "Is it all covered up?"

"I reckon the ingin's out o' the snow. She's steamin' and of course she'd melt the snow about her boiler and stack," the farmer said. "But I didn't look that way."

"Say!" demanded Bess, with some eagerness. "Is that Peleg's house near?"

"Peleg Morton? Why, 'tain't much farther than ye kin hear a pig's whisper," said Mr. Snubbins. "I'm goin' right there, myself. My woman wants ter know is Celia all right. She's some worried, 'cause Celia went over to visit Peleg's gal airly yesterday mornin' an' we ain't seen Celia since."

Mr. Carter came back with one of the brakemen just then, bearing a can of milk. The kindly conductor had found a tin plate, too—a section of the fireman's dinner kettle—and into this he poured some of the milk for the hungry little spaniel.

"There you are, Buster," he said, patting the dog, beside which Nan knelt to watch the process of consumption—for the puppy was so hungry that he tried to get nose, ears and fore-paws right in the dish!

"You're awfully kind," Nan said to Mr. Carter. "Now the little fellow will be all right."

"You better get him out of the way of that fat man," advised the conductor. "He owns the dog, you know. Bulson, I mean. He's forward in the other car, gourmandizing himself on a jar of condensed milk. I let him have one can; but I'm going to hold the rest against emergency. Now that the snow has stopped falling," he added cheerfully, as he passed on, "they ought to get help to us pretty soon."

The puppy was ready to cuddle down in his carrier and go to sleep when he had lapped up the milk. Nan wiped his silky ears with her pocket handkerchief, and his cunning little muzzle as well, and left him with a pat to go and seek Bess.

She found her chum still talking with Mr. Snubbins in the opening between the two cars. "Oh, Nan!" cried the impulsive one, rushing to meet her chum. "What do you think?"

"On what subject, young lady—on what subject?" demanded Nan, in her most dictatorial way, and aping one of the teachers at Lakeview Hall.

"On the subject of eats!" laughed Bess.

"Oh, my dear! Don't talk about it, please! If you drew a verbal picture of a banquet right now," Nan declared, "I'd eat it, verb and all."

"Do be sane and sensible," said Bess, importantly. "We're going out to supper. Now, wait! don't faint, Nan. This Mr. Snubbins is a dear! Why, he is a regular angel with chin whiskers—nothing less."

"He's never invited us to his house for supper?"

"No. His home is too far. But he says we can come along with him to Peleg's house and they will welcome us there. They are very hospitable people, these Mortons, so our angel says. And he and his daughter, Celia, will come back with us. And we can buy something there at the Mortons' to help feed the hungry children aboard the train."

That last appealed to Nan Sherwood, if nothing else did. There was but a single doubt in her mind.

"Oh, Bess!" she cried. "Do you think we ought to go? Shouldn't we ask permission?"

"Of whom?" demanded Bess, in surprise. "Surely the train won't steam off and leave us," and she broke into a laugh. "Oh, come on,

Miss Fussbudget! Don't be afraid. I've been asking permission a dozen times a day for more than three months. I'm glad to do something 'off my own bat,' as my brother Billy says. Come on, Nan."

So Nan went. They found Mr. Si Snubbins, "the angel with chin whiskers," ready to depart. He climbed up first and got upon the crust of the snow; then he helped both girls to mount to his level. So another adventure for Nan and Bess began.

CHAPTER X

THE RUNAWAYS

The almost level rays of a sinking sun shone upon a vast waste of white when the two girls from the snow-bound train started off with the farmer toward the only sign of life to be seen upon the landscape—a curl of blue smoke rising from a chimney of a farmhouse.

"That's Peleg's place," explained Mr. Snubbins. "He's a right well-to-do man, Peleg Morton is. We don't mind havin' our Celia go so much with Sallie Morton—though her mother does say that Sallie puts crazy notions into our Celia's head. But I reckon all gals is kinder crazy, ain't they?" pursued the farmer, with one of his sly glances and chuckles.

"Always!" agreed Bess, heartily. "Half of our girls at Lakeview Hall have to be kept in straightjackets, or padded cells."

"Mercy, Bess!" whispered Nan. "That's worthy of extravagant Laura Polk herself."

"Thank you," responded Bess, as the farmer recovered from a fit of "the chuckles" over Bess Harley's joke. Bess added this question:

"What particular form of insanity do your daughter and Sallie Morton display, Mr. Snubbins?"

"Movin' picters," ejaculated the farmer. "Drat 'em! They've jest about bewitched my gal and Sallie Morton."

"Goodness!" gasped Nan. "There aren't moving picture shows away out here in the country, are there?"

"Oncet a week at the Corner," said Mr. Snubbins. "An' we all go. But that ain't so much what's made Celia and Sallie so crazy. Ye see, las' fall was a comp'ny makin' picters right up here in Peleg's west parster. Goodness me! there was a crowd of 'em. They camped in tents like Gypsies, and they did the most amazin' things—they sure did!

"Dif'rent from Gypsies," pursued the farmer, "they paid for all they got around here. Good folks to sell chicken an' aigs to. City prices, we got," and Mr. Snubbins licked his lips like a dog in remembrance of a good meal.

"An' I vow ter Maria!" the man went on to say, with some eagerness. "We 'most all around here air in them picters; ya-as'm! Ye wouldn't think I was an actor, would ye?" And he went off into another spasm of chuckles.

"Oh, what fun!" cried Bess.

"Paid us two dollars a day for jest havin' our photographts took, they did," said Mr. Snubbins.

"And they paid three to the gals, 'cause they dressed up. That's what set Celia and Sallie by the ears. Them foolish gals has got it in their heads that they air jest cut out for movin' picter actresses. They wanter go off ter the city an' git jobs in one o' chem there studios! Peleg says he'll spank his gal, big as she is, if she don't stop sich foolish talk. I reckon Celia won't go fur without Sallie."

"My! it must be quite exciting to work for the pictures," said romantic Bess.

"Sure it is," chuckled the farmer. "One feller fell off a hoss while they was up here an' broke his collarbone; an' one of the gals tried ter milk our old Sukey from the wrong side, an' Sukey nigh kicked her through the side of the shed," and Mr. Snubbins indulged in another fit of laughter over this bit of comedy.

He was still chuckling when they climbed down from the hard eminence of a drift into a spot that had been cleared of snow before the Morton's side door. At once the door was opened and a big, bewhiskered man looked out.

"Well, well, Si!" he ejaculated. "I thought them was your Celia and my Sallie. *Them* girls air strangers, ain't they? Some more of that tribe of movin' picture actresses?"

"I vow ter Maria, Peleg!" ejaculated Mr. Snubbins. "What's happened to Celia? Ain't she here?"

"No. Nor no more ain't Sallie," Mr. Morton said. "Come in. Bring in them young ladies. I'll tell ye about it. Sallie's maw is mighty upsot."

"But ain't Celia *here*?" reiterated Mr. Snubbins, as he and the chums from Tillbury passed into the warm, big kitchen.

"No, she ain't, I tell you."

"But she started over for here yesterday morning, figgerin' to spend the day with your Sallie. When she didn't come back at night my woman an' me reckoned it snowed so hard you folks wouldn't let her come."

"Oh, lawk!" exclaimed Mr. Morton. "They was off yesterday mornin' just as soon as your Celia got here. Planned it all a forehand—the deceivin' imps! Said they was goin' to the Corner. An' they did! Sam Higgin picked 'em up there an' took 'em along to Littleton; an' when he plowed past here jest at evenin' through the snow he brought me a note. Hi, Maw, bring in that there letter," shouted Peleg Morton.

That the two men were greatly disturbed by the running away of their daughters, there could be no doubt. Nan was sorry she and Bess had come over from the train. These people were in serious trouble and she and her chum could not help them.

She drew the wondering Bess toward the door, and whispered: "What do you think, Bess? Can't we go back to the train alone?"

"What for, Nan?" cried Bess.

"Well, you see, they are in trouble."

At that moment Mrs. Morton hurried in with a fluttering sheet of paper in her hand. She was a voluminous woman in a stiffly starched house dress, everything about her as clean as a new pin, and a pair of silver-bowed spectacles pushed up to her fast graying hair. She was a wholesome, hearty, motherly looking woman, and Nan Sherwood was attracted to her at first sight.

Even usually unobservant Bess was impressed. "Isn't she a *love*?" she whispered to Nan.

"Poor woman!" Nan responded in the same tone, for there were undried tears on the cheeks of the farmer's wife.

"Here's Si, Maw," said Mr. Morton. "He ain't been knowin' about our girl and his Celia runnin' off, before."

"How do, Si?" responded Mrs. Morton. "Your wife'll be scairt ter death, I have no doubt. What'll become of them foolish girls—Why, Peke! who's these two young ladies?"

Mr. Morton looked to Mr. Snubbins for an introduction, scratching his head. Mr. Snubbins said, succinctly: "These here gals are from a railroad train that's snowed under down there in the cut. I expect they air hungry, Miz' Morton."

"Goodness me! Is that so?" cried the good woman, bustling forward and jerking her spectacles down astride her nose, the better to see the unexpected guests. "Snowed up—a whole train load, did you say? I declare! Sit down, do. I won't haf to put any extry plates on the supper table, for I *did* have it set, hopin' Sallie an' Celia would come back," and the poor mother began to sob openly.

"I vow, Maw! You *do* beat all. Them gals couldn't git back home through this snow, if they wanted to. And they likely got to some big town or other," said Mr. Morton, "before the worst of the blizzard. They've got money; the silly little tykes! When they have spent it all, they'll be glad to come back."

"Celia will, maybe," sobbed Mrs. Morton, brokenly. "She ain't got the determination of our Sallie. She'd starve rather than give in she was beat. We was too ha'sh with her, Paw. I feel we was too ha'sh! And maybe we won't never see our little gal again," and the poor lady sat down heavily in the nearest chair, threw her apron over her head, and cried in utter abandon.

CHAPTER XI

"A RURAL BEAUTY"

Nan Sherwood could not bear to see anybody cry. Her heart had already gone out to the farmer's wife whose foolish daughter had left home, and to see the good woman sobbing so behind her apron, won every grain of sympathy and pity in Nan's nature.

"Oh, you poor soul!" cried the girl, hovering over Mrs. Morton, and putting an arm across her broad, plump shoulders. "Don't cry—don't, don't cry! I'm *sure* the girls will come back. They are foolish to run away; but surely they will be glad to get back to their dear, dear homes."

"You don't know my Sallie," sobbed the woman.

"Oh! but she can't forget you—of course she can't," Nan said. "Why ever did they want to run away from home?"

"Them plagued movin' picters," Mr. Snubbins said gruffly, blowing his nose. "I don't see how I kin tell my woman about Celia."

"It was that there 'Rural Beauty' done it," Mr. Morton broke in peevishly. "Wish't I'd never let them film people camp up there on my paster lot and take them picters on my farm. Sallie was jest carried away with it. She acted in that five-reel film, 'A Rural Beauty.' And I must say she looked as purty as a peach in it."

"That's what they've run away for, I bet," broke in Si Snubbins. "Celia was nigh about crazy to see that picter run off. She was in it, too. Of course, a big drama like that wouldn't come to the Corner, and I shouldn't wonder if that's what took 'em both to the city, first of all. Still," he added, "I reckon they wanter be actorines, too."

Bess suppressed a giggle at that, for Si Snubbins was funny, whether intentionally so or not. Nan continued to try to soothe the almost hysterical Mrs. Morton. Mr. Morton said:

"Let's have that letter, Maw, that Sallie writ and sent back by Sam Higgins from Littleton."

Mrs. Morton reached out a hand blindly with the paper in it. Nan took it to give to Mr. Morton.

"You read it, Si," said Mr. Morton. "I ain't got my specs handy."

"Neither have I—and I ain't no hand to read writin' nohow," said his neighbor, honestly. "Here, young lady," to Nan. "Your eyes is better than ourn; you read it out to us."

Nan did as she was asked, standing beside Mrs. Morton's chair the while with a hand upon her shoulder:

"'Dear Maw and Paw:—

"'Celia and me have gone to the city and we are going to get jobs with the movies. We know we can—and make good, too. You tell Celia's Paw and Maw about her going with me. I'll take care of her. We've got plenty money—what with what we earned posing in those pictures in the fall, the Rural Beauty, and all. We will write you from where we are going, and you won't mind when you know how successful we are and how we are getting regular wages as movie actresses.

"'Good-bye, dear Paw and Maw, and a hundred kisses for Maw from

"'Your daughter,

"'Sallie Morton.

"'P.S.—I won't be known by my own name in the movies. I've picked a real nice sounding one, and so has Celia.'"

"There! You see?" said Mrs. Morton, who had taken the apron down so she could hear Nan the better. "We can't never trace 'em, because they'll be going by some silly names. Dear, dear me, Peke! Somethin' must be done."

"I dunno what, Maw," groaned the big man, hopelessly.

"What city have they gone to?" asked Bess, abruptly.

"Why, Miss," explained Mr. Morton, "they could go to half a dozen cities from Littleton. Of course they didn't stay there, although Littleton's a big town."

"Chicago?" queried Bess.

"Perhaps. But they could get to Detroit, or Indianapolis, or even to Cincinnati."

"There are more picture making concerns in Chicago," suggested Nan, quietly, "than in the other cities named, I am sure. And the fare to Chicago is less than to the others."

"Right you air, Miss!" agreed Si Snubbins. "That's where them pesky gals have set out for, I ain't a doubt."

"And how are we goin' to get 'em back?" murmured Mr. Morton.

"The good Lord won't let no harm come to the dears, I hope and pray," said his wife, wiping her eyes. "Somebody'll be good to 'em if they get sick or hungry. There! We ain't showin' very good manners to our guests, Peke. These girls are off that train where there ain't a bite to eat, I do suppose; and they must be half starved. Let's have supper. You pull up a chair, too, Si."

"All right, Miz' Morton," agreed Mr. Snubbins, briskly.

Nan felt some diffidence in accepting the good woman's hospitality. She whispered again to Bess:

"Shall we stay? They're in such trouble."

"But goodness!" interrupted Bess. "I'm hungry. And we want to get her interested in the kiddies aboard the train."

"Yes, that's so," agreed Nan.

"Come, girls," Mrs. Morton called from the other room. "Come right in and lay off your things—do. You are pretty dears—both of you. City girls, I'spect?"

"No, ma'am," Nan replied. "We live in a small town when we are at home. But we've been to boarding school and are on our way home for Christmas."

"And after that," Bess added briskly, "we're going to Chicago for two—whole—weeks!"

"You air? Well, well! D'you hear that, Peke?" as her husband came heavily into the room.

"What is it, Maw?"

"These girls are going to Chicago. If our Sallie and Si's Celia have gone there, mebbe these girls might come across them."

"Oh, Mrs. Morton!" cried Nan. "If we do, we will surely send them home to you. Or, if they are foolish enough not to want to come, we'll let you know at once where they are."

"Of course we will," agreed Bess.

"If you only had a picture of your daughter?" suggested Nan.

"Of Sallie? Why, we have," said Mrs. Morton. "She's some bigger now; but she had her photographt took in several 'poses', as they call 'em, when she was playin' in that 'Rural Beauty'. I got the prints myself from the man that took 'em."

But when she hunted for the pictures, Mrs. Morton found they were missing. "I declare for't!" she said, quite vexed. "I do believe that Sallie took 'em with her to show to folks she expects to ask for work. Jest like her! Oh, she's smart, Sallie is."

"There's that picter she had took the time we went to the County Fair, three year ago, Maw," suggested Mr. Morton, as they prepared to sit down to the bountiful table. "I 'low she's filled out some since then; she was as leggy as a colt. But these gals can see what she looks like in the face."

While he was speaking his wife brought forth the family album — a green plush affair with a huge gilt horseshoe on the cover. She turned over the leaves till she found Sallie's photograph, and displayed it with pride. Nan secretly thought her father's description of Sallie at twelve years old or so was a very good one; but Mrs. Morton evidently saw no defects in her child's personal appearance.

"Sallie wore her hair in curls then, you see," said Mrs. Morton. "But she says they ain't fashionable now, and she's been windin' her braids into eartabs like that leadin' lady in the movie company done. Makes Sallie look dreadfully growed up," sighed the troubled woman. "I sartainly do hate to see my little girl change into a woman so quick."

"That's what my woman says," agreed Snubbins. "Celia's 'bout growed up, she thinks. But I reckon if her mother laid her across her lap like she uster a few years back, she could nigh about slap most of the foolishness out o' Celia. Gals nowadays git to feel too big for their boots—that's what the matter."

"Mercy!" gasped Bess. "I hope my mother won't go back to first principles with me, if I displease her. And I'm sure your Celia can't be really bad."

"Just foolish—just foolish, both on 'em," Mr. Morton said. "Let me help you again."

"Oh, I'm so full," sighed Bess.

"I'm afraid ye ain't makin' out a supper," Mrs. Morton said.

"Indeed we are," cried Nan. "I only wish the children on that snowbound train had some of these good things."

This turned the current of conversation and the Mortons were soon interested in the girls' story of the castaways in the snow. Mrs. Morton set to work at once and packed two big baskets with food. A whole ham that she had boiled that day was made into sandwiches. There were hard boiled eggs, and smoked beef and cookies, pies and cakes. In fact, the good woman stripped her pantry for the needy people in the stalled train.

Her husband got into his outer garments and helped Si Snubbins carry the baskets across the snow. Mrs. Morton's last words to the girls were:

"Do, *do*, my dears, try to find my girl and Celia when you go to Chicago."

Nan and Bess promised to do so, for neither realized what a great city Chicago is, and that people might live there, almost side by side, for years and never meet.

CHAPTER XII

RAVELL BULSON'S TROUBLE

"What do you think of those two girls, anyway, Nan?" Bess Harley asked.

This was late in the evening, after the porter had made up their berths again in the Pullman. The baskets of food had been welcomed by the snow-bound passengers with acclaim. The two girls were thanked more warmly for their thoughtfulness than Nan and Bess believed they really deserved.

Bess Harley's question, of course, referred to Sallie Morton and Celia Snubbins, the girls who had run away from home to become moving picture actresses. Nan replied to her chum's query:

"That Sallie Morton must be a very silly girl indeed to leave such a comfortable home and such a lovely mother. Perhaps Celia Snubbins may not have been so pleasantly situated; but I am sure she had no reason for running away."

Bess sighed. "Well," she murmured, "it must be great fun to work for the movies. Just think of those two country girls appearing in a five-reel film like 'A Rural Beauty.'"

"Well, for goodness' sake, Bess Harley!" cried Nan, astonished, "have you been bitten by *that* bug?"

"Don't call it 'bug'—that sounds so common," objected Bess. "Call it 'bacilli of the motion picture.' It must be *great*," she added emphatically, "to see yourself acting on the screen!"

"I guess so," Nan said, with a laugh. "A whole lot those two foolish girls *acted* in that 'Rural Beauty' picture. They were probably two of the 'merry villagers' who helped to make a background for the real actresses. You know very well, Bess, that girls like us wouldn't be hired by any film company for anything important."

"Why—you know, Nan," her chum said, "that some of the most highly paid film people are young girls."

"Yes. But they are particularly fitted for the work. Do you feel the genius of a movie actress burning in you?" scoffed Nan.

"No-o," admitted Bess. "I think it is that hard boiled egg I ate. And it doesn't exactly burn."

Nan went off in a gale of laughter at this, and stage-struck Bess chimed in. "I don't care," the latter repeated, the last thing before they climbed into their respective berths, "it must be oodles of fun to work for the movies."

While the chums slept there were great doings outside the snow-bound train. The crew turned out with shovels, farmers in the neighborhood helped, and part of a lately arrived section gang joined in to shovel the snow away from the stalled engine and train.

Cordwood had been bought of Peleg Morton and hauled over to the locomotive for fuel. With this the engineer and fireman managed to make sufficient steam to heat the Pullman coach and the smoking car. Nan and Bess had brought little "Buster," as the spaniel had been named, into their section and, having been fed and made warm, he gave the girls hardly any trouble during the night.

Selfish Mr. Bulson, who had shipped the puppy home to his little boy, seemed to have no interest whatsoever in Buster's welfare.

It was not until the great snow-plow and a special locomotive appeared the next morning, and towed the stalled train on to its destination, and Nan Sherwood and her chum arrived at Tillbury, that Nan learned anything more regarding Mr. Ravell Bulson.

Mr. and Mrs. Sherwood had been more than a little worried by Nan's delay in getting home and Mr. Sherwood was at the station to meet the train when it finally steamed into Tillbury.

Owneyville, which the girls knew to be Mr. Bulson's home town, was a station beyond Tillbury, and a much smaller town. The fat man had to change cars, so it was not surprising that he stepped down upon the Tillbury platform just as Nan ran into her father's arms.

"Oh, Papa Sherwood!" Nan almost sobbed.

"My dear Nancy!" he returned, quite as much moved.

And just then Mr. Bulson appeared beside them. "Well, Sherwood!" the fat man growled, "have you come to your senses yet?"

Robert Sherwood's face flushed and he urged Nan away along the snowy platform. "I don't care to talk to you, Bulson," he said shortly.

"Well, you *will* talk to me!" exclaimed the angry fat man. "I'll get you into court where you'll have to talk."

Mr. Sherwood kept right on with Nan and Bulson was left fuming and muttering on the platform. Bess had already been put into the family sleigh and was being whisked home. Nan and her father tramped briskly through the snowy streets toward "the little dwelling in amity," which Nan had not seen since leaving Tillbury for her Uncle Henry Sherwood's home at Pine Camp, ten months before.

"Oh, *dear*, Papa Sherwood!" gasped Nan. "What is the matter with that horrid man? He says the most dreadful things about you!"

"What's that?" demanded her father, quickly. "What do you know about Bulson?"

"More than I really want to know about him," said Nan, ruefully. She related briefly what had happened a few days before on Pendragon Hill. "And when he called you a rascal, I—oh! I was very, very angry! What did he mean, Papa Sherwood?"

But her father postponed his explanation until later; and it was really from her mother that Nan heard the story of Mr. Sherwood's trouble with Ravell Bulson. Mrs. Sherwood was very indignant about it, and so, of course, was Nan.

A week or more before, Mr. Sherwood had had business in Chicago, and in returning took the midnight train. The sleeping car was sidetracked at Tillbury and when most of the passengers were gone the man in the berth under Mr. Sherwood's began to rave about having been robbed. His watch and roll of banknotes had disappeared.

The victim of the robbery was Mr. Ravell Bulson. Mr. Bulson had at once accused the person occupying the berth over his as being the guilty person. Nan's father had got up early, and had left the sleeping car long before Mr. Bulson discovered his loss.

The railroad and the sleeping car company, of course, refused to acknowledge responsibility for Mr. Bulson's valuables. Nor on mere suspicion could Mr. Bulson get a justice in Tillbury to issue a warrant for Mr. Sherwood.

But Ravell Bulson had been to the Sherwood cottage on Amity Street, and had talked very harshly. Besides, the fat man had in public loudly accused his victim of being dishonest.

Mr. Sherwood's reputation for probity in Tillbury was well founded; he was liked and respected; those who really knew him would not be influenced by such a scandal.

But as Mr. Sherwood was making plans to open an agency in Tillbury for a certain automobile manufacturing concern, he feared that the report of Mr. Bulson's charge would injure his usefulness to the corporation he was about to represent. To sue Bulson for slander would merely give wider circulation to the story the fat man had originated.

Ravell Bulson was a traveling man and was not often in Tillbury — that was one good thing. He had a reputation in his home town of Owneyville of being a quarrelsome man, and was not well liked by his neighbors.

Nevertheless a venomous tongue can do a great deal of harm, and a spiteful enemy may sometimes bring about a greater catastrophe than a more powerful adversary.

CHAPTER XIII

ADVENTURES IN A GREAT CITY

"Now! what *do* you know about this?" Bess Harley demanded, with considerable vexation.

"Of course, it's a mistake—or else that big clock's wrong," declared Nan Sherwood.

"No fear of a railroad clock's being wrong," said her chum, grumpily. "That old time table was wrong. *They're* always wrong. No more sense to a time table than there is to a syncopated song. *It* said we were to arrive in this station three-quarters of an hour ago—and it turns out that it meant an entirely different station and an entirely different train."

Nan laughed rather ruefully. "I guess it is our own fault and not the time table's. But the fact remains that we are in the wrong place, and at the wrong time. Walter and Grace, of course, met that other train and, not finding us, will have gone home, not expecting us till to-morrow."

"Goodness, what a pickle!" Bess complained. "And how will we find the Mason's house, Nan Sherwood?"

The chums had the number and street of their friends' house, but it occurred to neither of them to go to a telephone booth and call up the house, stating the difficulty they were in. Nor did the girls think of asking at the information bureau, or even questioning one of the uniformed policemen about the huge station.

"Now, of course," Nan said firmly, "some street car must go within walking distance of Grace's house."

"Of course, but which car?" demanded Bess.

"That is the question, isn't it?" laughed Nan.

"One of these taxi-cabs could take us," suggested Bess.

"But they cost so much," objected her friend. "And we can't read those funny clocks they have and the chauffeur could overcharge us all he pleased. Besides," Nan added, "I don't like their looks."

"Looks of what—the taxis?"

"The chauffeurs," responded Nan, promptly.

"We-ell, we've got to go somehow—and trust to somebody," Bess said reflectively. "I wonder should we go to that hotel where we stayed that week with mother? They would take us in I suppose."

"But goodness! why should we be so helpless?" demanded Nan. "I'm sure two boys would start right out and find their way to Grace's."

"Would you *dare*?" cried Bess.

"Why not? Come on! We don't want to spend all our money in taxi fares. Let's go over there and ask that car man who seems to be bossing the conductors and motormen."

The girls, with their handbags, started across the great square before the station. Almost at once they found themselves in a tangle of vehicular traffic that quite confused Bess, and even troubled the cooler-headed Nan.

"Oh, Nan! I'm scared!" cried her chum, clinging with her free hand to Nan's arm.

"For pity's sake, don't be foolish!" commanded Nan. "You'll get me excited, too—Oh!"

An automobile swept past, so near the two girls that the step brushed their garments. Bess almost swooned. Nan wished with all her heart that they had not so recklessly left the sidewalk.

Suddenly a shrill voice cried at her elbow: "Hi, greeny! you look out, now, or one of these horses will take a bite out o' you. My! but you're the green goods, for fair."

Nan turned to look, expecting to find a saucy street boy; but the owner of the voice was a girl. She was dirty-faced, undersized, poorly dressed, and ill-nourished. But she was absolutely independent, and stood there in the crowded square with all the assurance of a traffic policeman.

"Come on, greenies," urged this strange little mortal (she could not have been ten years old), "and I'll beau you over the crossing myself. Something'll happen to you if you take root here."

She carried in a basket on her arm a few tiny bunches of stale violets, each bunch wrapped in waxed paper to keep it from the frost. Nan had seen dozens of these little flower-sellers of both sexes on the street when she had passed through Chicago with her Uncle Henry the winter before.

"Oh, let's go with her," cried the quite subdued Bess. "Do, Nan!"

It seemed rather odd for these two well-dressed and well-grown girls to be convoyed by such a "hop-o'-my-thumb" as the flower-seller. But the latter got Nan and Bess to an "isle of safety" in a hurry, and would then have darted away into the crowd without waiting to be thanked, had not Nan seized the handle of her basket.

"Wait!" she cried. "Don't run away."

"Hey!" said the flower-seller, "I ain't got time to stop and chin-chin. I got these posies to sell."

"Sell us two," Nan commanded. "Wait!"

"Aw right. 'F you say so," said the small girl. "Fifteen a bunch," she added quickly, shrewdly increasing by a nickel the regular price of the stale boutonnières.

Nan opened her purse to pay for both. Bess said, rather timidly: "I should think you would be afraid of getting run over every time you cross the street—you're so little."

"Aw—say!" responded the strange girl, quite offended. "What d'ye think I am—a *kid*? I live here, I do! I ain't country, and don't know me way 'round."

"Meaning that we *are*, I suppose?" laughed Nan.

"Well," drawled the girl, "it sticks out all over you. I can tell 'em a block away. An' I bet you're lost and don't know where you're goin'. You two didn't come here to be pitcher actors, did ye?"

"Why—no!" gasped Bess.

Nan was moved to ask. "What put that idea in your head, honey?"

"I guess 'most girls that run away from home nowadays are lookin' to make a hit in the pitchers—ain't they?"

"You ridiculous child, you!" laughed Bess. "We haven't run away."

"No? Well, I thought mebbe youse did," said the flower-seller, grinning impishly. "I see a plenty of 'em comin' off the trains, I do."

"Runaway girls?" cried Nan,

"They don't tell me they have run away. But they are all greenies—just as green as grass," this shrewd child of the street declared.

"Have you seen any girls lately who have come to the city to be picture actresses?" Nan asked with sudden eagerness.

"Yep," was the reply.

"Sure?" cried Bess. "You don't mean it!"

"Yes, I do. Two girls bigger'n you. Le's see—it was last Friday."

"The second day of the big blizzard?" cried Nan.

"That's the very day," agreed Bess. "It's when Sallie and Celia would have got here if they *were* coming to Chicago."

"Hi!" exclaimed the flower girl. "What's you talkin' about? Who's Sallie and Celia?"

"Girls whom we think came to the city the other day just as you said," Nan explained. "They have run away to be moving picture actresses."

"Hi!" exclaimed the flower-seller again. "What sort o' lookin' girls?"

"Why—I don't know exactly," confessed Nan. "Do we, Bess? Mrs. Morton said Sallie took with her those photographs that were taken while the girls were playing as extras in 'A Rural Beauty.'"

"That's it!" suddenly interrupted the flower-girl. "I bet I seen those two. They didn't call each other 'Sallie' and 'Celia'; but they had some fancy names—I forgot what."

"Oh! are you *sure*?" cried Bess.

> "They had them photographs just like you say. They showed 'em to me. You see," said the little girl, "I showed 'em where they could eat cheap, and they told me how they was going to join a movie company."

CHAPTER XIV

THE FIRST CLUE

Nan and her chum were wildly excited. During their brief stay at Tillbury over Christmas they had been so busy, at home and abroad, that they had not thought much about Sallie Morton and Celia Snubbins, the two runaways.

In Nan's case, not having seen her mother for ten months, she did not—at the last moment—even desire to come away from her and visit her school friends in Chicago.

There really was so much to say, so much to learn about Scotland and the beautiful old Emberon Castle and the village about it, and about the queer people Mrs. Sherwood had met, too! Oh! Nan hoped that she would see the place in time—the "Cradle of the Blake Clan," as Mr. Sherwood called it.

There had been presents, of course, and in the giving and accepting of these Nan had found much pleasure and excitement—especially when she found a box of beautiful new clothes for her big doll, all made in Scotland by "Momsey," who knew just how precious Beautiful Beulah was in her daughter's eyes.

With all her work and play at Lakeview Hall, Nan Sherwood had not forgotten Beulah. The other girls of her age and in her grade were inclined to laugh at Nan for playing dolls; but at the last of the term Beautiful Beulah had held the post of honor in Room Seven, Corridor Four.

Nan's love for dolls foreshadowed her love for babies. She never could pass a baby by without trying to make friends with it. The little girls at Lakeview Hall found a staunch friend and champion in Nan Sherwood. It was a great grief to Mrs. Sherwood and Nan that there were no babies in the "little dwelling in amity." Nan could barely remember the brother that had come to stay with them such a little while, and then had gone away forever.

Nan's heart was touched by the apparent needs of this street girl who had come to the rescue of Bess and herself when they arrived in

Chicago. All the time she and her chum were trying to learn something about the two girls who had come to the great city to be moving picture actresses, and listening to what the flower-seller had to say about them, Nan was thinking, too, of their unfortunate little informant.

"Is that restaurant where you took those girls to eat near here?" she suddenly asked.

"Aw, say! 'tain't no rest'rant," said the child. "It's just Mother Beasley's hash-house."

"Goodness!" gasped Bess. "Is it a *nice* place?"

The girl grinned. "'Cordin' ter what you thinks is nice. I 'spect *you'd* like the Auditorium Annex better. But Mother Beasley's is pretty good when you ain't got much to spend."

Bess looked at Nan curiously. The latter was eager to improve this acquaintanceship so strangely begun, and for more than one reason.

"Could you show us to Mother Beasley's—if it isn't very far away?" Nan asked.

"Aw, say! What d'ye think? I ain't nawthan' ter do but beau greenies around this burg? A swell chaunc't I'd have to git any eats meself. I gotter sell these posies, I have."

"But you can eat with us!" Nan suggested.

"Oh, Nan!" Bess whispered. "Do you s'pose we can find any clue to those girls there?"

"I hope so," returned Nan, in the same low voice.

"Goodness! I'm just as excited as I can be," her chum went on to say. "We'll be regular detectives. *This* beats being a movie actress, right now."

Nan smiled, but in a moment was grave again. "I'd do a great deal for that lovely Mrs. Morton," she said. "And even funny old Si Snubbins had tears in his eyes at the last when he begged us to find his Celia."

"I know it," Bess agreed sympathetically. "But I can't help being excited just the same. If we should find them at this Mother Beasley's—"

"I don't expect that; but we may hear of them there," said Nan. "Here's our new chum."

The flower-girl had darted away to sell one of her little bouquets. Now she came back and took up the discussion where she had dropped it.

"Now about those eats," she said. "I ain't in the habit of eating at all hours; it don't agree wid my constitootin, me doctor tells me. Fact is, sometimes I don't eat much, if *any*."

"Oh!" gasped Bess.

"That's when I don't sell out. An' I got five posies left. I b'lieve I'd better take ye up on this offer. Youse pay for me feed for the pleasure of me comp'ny; hey?"

"That's the answer," said Nan, spiritedly. "We're going to be good friends, I can see."

"We are if youse is goin' to pay for me eats," agreed the girl.

"What is your name?" asked Nan, as their young pilot guided the chums across to the opening of a side-street. "Mine is Nan, and my friend's is Bess."

"Well, they calls me some mighty mean names sometimes; but my real, honest-to-goodness name is Inez. Me mudder was a Gypsy Queen and me fadder was boss of a section gang on de railroad somewhere. He went off and me mudder died, and I been livin' with me aunt. She's good enough when she ain't got a bottle by her, and me and her kids have good times. But I gotter rustle for me own grub. We all haster."

Nan and Bess listened to this, and watched the independent little thing in much amazement. Such a creature neither of the chums from Tillbury had ever before heard of or imagined.

"Do you suppose she is telling the truth?" whispered Bess to Nan.

"I don't see why she should tell a wrong story gratuitously," Nan returned.

"Come on, girls," said Inez, turning into another street—narrower and more shabby than the first. "Lift your feet! I ain't got no time to waste."

Nan laughed and hastened her steps; but Bess looked doubtful.

"Hi!" exclaimed the street girl, "are you sure you two ain't wantin' to break into the movies, too?"

"Not yet," proclaimed Nan. "But we would like to find a couple of girls who, I think, came to Chicago for that purpose."

"Hi! them two I was tellin' you about?"

"Perhaps."

"Their folks want 'em back?" asked the street child, abruptly.

"I should say they did!" cried Bess.

"Ain't they the sillies!" exclaimed Inez. "Catch me leavin' a place where they didn't beat me too much and where the eats came reg'lar."

"Oh!" again ejaculated Bess.

Just then a little boy, more ragged even than their guide, approached. At once Inez proceeded to shove him off the sidewalk, and when he objected, she slapped him soundly.

"Why, goodness me, child!" cried the astonished Nan, "what did you do that for? Did he do anything to you?"

"Nope. Never seen him before," admitted Inez. "But I pitch into all the boys I see that I'm sure I can whip. Then they let me alone. They think I'm tough. These boys wouldn't let a girl sell a flower, nor a newspaper, nor nothin', if they could help it. We girls got ter fight 'em."

"The beginning of suffragism," groaned Nan.

"I never heard of such a thing!" Bess cried. "Fighting the boys—how disgraceful!"

Inez stared at her. "Hi!" she finally exclaimed, "you wouldn't make much if you didn't fight, I can tell ye. When I see a boy with a basket of posies, I pull it away from him and tear 'em up. Boys ain't got no business selling posies around here. That's a girl's job, and I'm goin' to show 'em, I am!"

Nan and Bess listened to this with mingled emotions. It was laughable, yet pitiful. Little boys and girls fighting like savages for a bare existence. The chums were silent the rest of the way to the old brick house—just a "slice" out of a three-story-and-basement row of such houses, which Inez announced to be "Mother Beasley's."

"Sometimes she's got her beds all full and you hafter wait for lodgin's. Mebbe she'll let you camp in her room, or in one of the halls up-stairs."

"Oh, but, my dear, we don't wish to stay!" Nan said. "Only to eat here and inquire about those other girls."

"Where' ye goin' to stop?" asked Inez, curiously.

"We have friends out by Washington Park," Bess said. "They'd have met us, only there was some mistake in the arrival of our train."

"Hi! Washington Park?" exclaimed the flower-seller. "Say, you must be big-bugs."

Nan laughed. "I guess *they* are," she said.

"Youse won't be suited with Mother Beasley's grub," said the girl, hesitating at the basement steps.

"I believe she's right," Bess said faintly, as the odor of cooking suddenly burst forth with the opening of the door under the long flight leading to the front door of the house.

"I've eaten in a lumber camp," said Nan, stoutly. "I'm sure this can't be as hard."

CHAPTER XV

CONTRASTS

A girl not much bigger than Inez, nor dressed much better, came out of the basement door of Mother Beasley's, wiping her lips on the back of her hand.

"Hullo, Ine!" she said to the flower-seller. "Who you got in tow? Some more greenies."

"Never you mind, Polly," returned Inez. "They're just friends of mine—on their way to Washington Park."

"Yes—they—be!" drawled the girl called Polly.

"Hi! that's all right," chuckled Inez. "I t'ought I'd make ye sit up and take notice. But say! wot's good on the menu ter-day?"

"Oh, say! take me tip," said Polly. "Order two platters of Irish stew an' a plate o' ham an' eggs. Youse'll have a bully feed then. Eggs is cheap an' Mother Beasley's givin' t'ree fer fifteen cents, wid the ham throwed in. That'll give youse each an egg an' plenty of stew in the two platters for all t'ree."

This arrangement of a course dinner on so economical a plan made Bess open her eyes, while Nan was greatly amused.

"How strong's the bank?" asked Inez of Nan, whom she considered the leader of the expedition. "Can we stand fifteen cents apiece?"

"I think so," returned the girl from Tillbury, gravely.

"Good as gold, then!" their pilot said. "We'll go to it. By-by, Polly!"

She marched into the basement. Bess would never have dared proceed that far had it not been for Nan's presence.

A woman with straggling gray hair met them at the door of the long dining-room. She had a tired and almost toothless smile; but had it not been for her greasy wrapper, uncombed hair and grimy nails, Mother Beasley might have been rather attractive.

"Good afternoon, dearies," she said. "Dinner's most over; but maybe we can find something for you. You goin' to eat, Inez?"

"Ev'ry chance't I get," declared the flower-seller, promptly.

"Sit right down," said Mrs. Beasley, pointing to the end of a long table, the red-and-white cloth of which was stained with the passage of countless previous meals, and covered with the crumbs from "crusty" bread.

Bess looked more and more doubtful. Nan was more curious than she was hungry. Inez sat down promptly and began scraping the crumbs together in a little pile, which pile when completed, she transferred to the oil-cloth covered floor with a dexterous flip of the knife.

"Come on!" she said. "Shall I order for youse?"

"We are in your hands, Inez," declared Nan, gravely. "Do with us as you see fit."

"Mercy!" murmured Bess, sitting down gingerly enough, after removing her coat in imitation of her chum.

"Hi!" shouted Inez, in her inimitable way. "Hi, Mother Beasley! bring us two orders of the Irish and one ham an' eggs. Like 'em sunny-side up?"

"Like *what* sunny-side up?" gasped Bess.

"Yer eggs."

"Which is the sunny-side of an egg?" asked Bess faintly, while Nan was convulsed with laughter.

"Hi!" ejaculated Inez again. "Ain't you the greenie? D'ye want yer egg fried on one side, or turned over?"

"Turned over," Bess murmured.

"An' you?" asked the flower-seller of Nan.

"I always like the sunny-side of everything," our Nan admitted.

"Hi, Mother Beasley!" shouted Inez, to the woman in the kitchen. "Two of them eggs sunny-side up, flop the other."

Nan burst out laughing again at this. Bess was too funny for anything—to look at!

There were other girls in the long room, but none near where Nan and Bess and their strange little friend sat. Plainly the strangers were working girls, somewhat older than the chums, and as they finished their late dinners, one by one, they went out. Some wore cheap finery, but most of them showed the shabby hall-mark of poverty in their garments.

By and by the steaming food appeared. Inez had been helping herself liberally to bread and butter and the first thing Mother Beasley did was to remove the latter out of the flower-seller's reach.

"It's gone up two cents a pound," she said plaintively. "But if it was a dollar a pound some o' you girls would never have no pity on neither the bread nor the butter."

The stew really smelled good. Even Bess tried it with less doubt. Inez ate as though she had fasted for a week and never expected to eat again.

"Will you have coffee, dearies?" asked Mother Beasley.

"Three cents apiece extry," said Inez, hoarsely.

"Yes, please," Nan said. "And if there is pie, we will have pie."

"Oh, you pie!" croaked Inez, aghast at such recklessness. "I reckon you *do* 'blong up to Washington Park."

Nan had to laugh again at this, and even Bess grew less embarrassed. When Mrs. Beasley came back with the coffee and pie, Nan drew her into conversation.

"Inez, here, says she introduced two other girls from the country to your home a few days ago," said Nan. "Two girls who were looking for jobs with the movies."

"Were they?" asked Mrs. Beasley, placidly. "My girls are always looking for jobs. When they get 'em, if they are good jobs, they go to live where the accommodations are better. I do the best I can for 'em; but I only accommodate poor girls."

"And I think you really must do a great deal of good, in your way, Mrs. Beasley," Nan declared. "Did these two we speak of chance to stay with you until now?"

"I was thinkin'," said Mrs. Beasley. "I know, now, the ones you mean. Yes, Inez *did* bring 'em. But they only stayed one night. They wus used to real milk, and real butter, and strictly fresh eggs, and feather beds. They was real nice about it; but I showed 'em how I couldn't give 'em live-geese feather beds an' only charge 'em a dollar apiece a week for their lodgin's.

"They had money—or 'peared to have. And they heard the movin' picture studios were all on the other side of town. So they went away."

"Oh, dear!" sighed Bess.

"Well, they were all right at that time. I'll write and tell Mrs. Morton," Nan said.

"Did they tell you their names, Mrs. Beasley?" she asked.

"Bless you! if they did, I don't remember. I have twenty-five girls all the time and lots of 'em only stay a few nights. I couldn't begin to keep track of 'em, or remember their names."

This was all the information the chums could get from Mrs. Beasley regarding the girls whom Nan and Bess believed to be the runaways. A little later they went out with Inez, the latter evidently filled to repletion.

"Hi! but that *was* a feed! You girls must be millionaires' daughters, like the newspapers tell about," said the street girl.

"Oh, no, we're not," Nan cried.

"Well, you better be joggin' along toward Washington Park. I don't want youse should get robbed while I'm with you. Mebbe the police'd think I done it."

"If you will put us on the car that goes near this address," said Nan, seriously, showing Inez Walter Mason's card, "we'll be awfully obliged."

Inez squinted at the address. "I kin do better'n that," she declared. "I'll put youse in a jitney that'll drop ye right at the corner of the street—half a block away."

"Oh! a jitney!" Bess cried. "Of course."

Inez marched them a couple of blocks and there, on a busy corner, hailed the auto-buss. Before this Nan had quietly obtained from the child her home address and the name of her aunt.

"In you go," said the flower-seller. Then she shouted importantly to the 'bus-driver: "I got your number, mister! You see't these ladies gets off at their street or you'll get deep into trouble. Hear me?"

"Sure, Miss! Thank ye kindly, Miss," said the chauffeur, saluting, with a grin, and the jitney staggered on over the frozen snow and ice of the street.

They came to the Mason house, safe and sound. An important-looking man in a tail coat and an imposing shirt-front let the girls into the great house.

"Yes, Miss," he said, in answer to Nan's inquiry. "There must have been some mistake, Miss. Miss Grace and Mister Walter went to the station to meet you, and returned long ago. I will tell them you have arrived."

He turned away in a stately manner, and Bess whispered: "I feel just as countrified as that little thing said we looked."

Nan was looking about the reception room and contrasting its tasteful richness with Mother Beasley's place.

CHAPTER XVI

A SPIN IN THE PARK

Grace's home was a beautiful, great house, bigger than the Harley's at Tillbury, and Nan Sherwood was impressed by its magnificence and by the spacious rooms. Her term at Lakeview Hall had made Nan much more conversant with luxury than she had been before. At home in the little cottage on the by-street, although love dwelt there, the Sherwoods had never lived extravagantly in any particular. Mrs. Sherwood's long invalidism had eaten up the greater part of Mr. Sherwood's salary when he worked in the Atwater Mills; and now that Mrs. Sherwood's legacy from her great uncle, Hugh Blake of Emberon, was partly tied up in the Scotch courts, the Sherwoods would continue to limit their expenditures.

At Mrs. Sherwood's urgent request, her husband was going into the automobile business. A part of the money they had brought back from Scotland had already been used in fitting up a handsome showroom and garage on the main street of Tillbury; and some other heavy expenses had fallen upon Mr. Sherwood, for which he would, however, be recompensed by the sale of the first few cars.

If Ravell Bulson injured Mr. Sherwood's business reputation by his wild charges, or if the company Mr. Sherwood expected to represent, heard of the trouble, much harm might be done. The automobile manufacturing company might even refuse to allow their cars to be handled by Mr. Sherwood—which was quite within their rights, according to the contract which had been signed between them.

Enough of this, however. Nan and Bess Harley were established with Grace Mason, in Chicago, expecting to have a fine time. Nan tried to put all home troubles off her mind.

The girls occupied a beautiful large suite together on the third floor, with a bath all their own, and a maid to wait upon them. Grace was used to this; but she was a very simple-minded girl, and the presence of a tidy, be-aproned and be-capped maid not much older than herself, did not particularly impress Grace one way or another.

"I feel like a queen," Bess confessed, luxuriously. "I can say: 'Do thus and so,' and 'tis done. I might say: 'Off with his head!' if one of my subjects displeased me, and he would be guillotined before you could wink an eye."

"How horrid!" said Grace, the shy. "I never could feel that way."

"It would never do for Elizabeth to be a grand vizer, or sultan, or satrap," Nan remarked laughingly.

"Who wants to be a 'shawl-strap'? Not I!" cried Bess, gaily. "I am Queen Bess, monarch of all I survey. Katie!"—the neat little maid had just entered the room—"will you hand me the book I was reading in the other room? I'm too weak to rise. Oh, thanks!"

Grace laughed; but Nan looked a little grave as Katie disappeared again.

"Don't, honey," Nan said to her thoughtless chum. "It isn't *nice*. The poor girl has necessary work enough without your making up thing's for her to do. She is on her feet from morning till night. She tells me that her ankles swell dreadfully sometimes, and that is awful for a young girl like her."

"Why, Nan!" Grace cried, "how did you know?"

"Katie told me," repeated Nan.

"But—but she never told me," expostulated their hostess.

"I don't suppose you ever saw her crying, as I did, while she was setting the dinner table. It was last evening. She had been on her feet more than usual yesterday. The doctor tells her that her arches are breaking down; but she cannot afford to have arch supports made at present, because her mother needs all the money Katie can earn."

"Mercy!" gasped Bess. "Did you ever see such a girl as Nan? She already knows all the private history of that girl."

"No, I do not," said Nan, with some indignation. "I never asked her a thing. She just told me. Lots of girls who have to go out to service are troubled with their arches breaking down. Especially when the floors are polished wood with nothing but rugs laid down. Bare floors may be very sanitary; but they are hard on the feet."

"There you go!" sighed Bess, "with a lot of erudite stuff that we don't understand. I wish you wouldn't."

"I know why Katie, and other people as well, love to tell Nan all their troubles," said Grace, softly. "Because she is sympathetic. I am afraid *I* ought to have known about poor Katie's feet."

The very next day the little serving maid was sent by Mrs. Mason to the orthopedic shoe shop to be measured for her arch supports and shoes. But it was Nan whom poor Katie caught alone in a dark corner of the hall when she came back, and humbly kissed.

"An' bless yer swate heart, Miss, for 'twas yer kind thought stirred up Miss Grace to tell the mistress. Bless yer swate heart again, I say!"

Nan kept this to herself, of course; but it pleased her very much that the word she had dropped had had such a splendid result. Grace, she knew, was a lovable girl and never exacting with the servants; and Mrs. Mason was good to her people, too. But it was a rather perfunctory sort of goodness, spurred by little real knowledge of their individual needs.

After this, it was quite noticeable that Grace was even more considerate of Katie and the other maids. Nan Sherwood had had little experience with domestic servants; but the appreciation of *noblesse oblige* was strong within her soul.

The girls' time, both day and evening, was fully occupied. The Masons' was a large household, and there seemed to be always company. It was almost like living in a hotel, only above and over all the freedom and gaiety of the life there, was the impression that it was a real *home*, and that the Mason family lived a very intimate existence, after all.

Walter and his father were close chums. Grace and her mother were like two very loving sisters. The smaller children were still with their governess and nurse most of the time. But there were times in every day when the whole family was together in private, with the rest of the household shut out.

There was always something going on for the young folk. The day's activities were usually planned at the general breakfast table. One day Nan had two hours of the forenoon on her hands, while her chum and Grace went shopping with Mrs. Mason. Nan did not like shopping—much.

"Not unless I can have lots of money in my pocket-book, and be extravagant," she said, laughing.

"You never were extravagant in your life!" declared Bess, in refutation of this.

However, Nan was left alone and Walter found it out. He had brought his black horse down from Freeling with him. He sent for this and the cutter, and insisted that Nan go with him through the park.

Nan went, and would have had a delightful time had it not been for a single incident. As they turned back, suddenly there met them a very handsome, heavy, family sleigh, the pair of horses jingling their harness-bells proudly, and with tossing plumes and uniformed coachman and footman.

"Goodness!" gasped Nan, as she saw a girl in furs lean far out of the great sleigh and wave her muff to Walter.

It was Linda Riggs. Linda quite ignored Nan's presence behind the black horse.

CHAPTER XVII

"A MOVING SCENE"

Nan did not refuse to go shopping every time her school friends went. The big Chicago stores appealed to her just as much as to any country girl who ever fell under their charm. In the Windy City the department stores—that mammoth of modern commerce—is developed to the highest degree.

It was like wandering through an Alladin's Palace for Nan to walk about Wilson-Meadows, Galsig-Wheelwrights, or any of the other big stores. And it was because she was so much interested in what she saw, that she wandered one day away from her friends and found herself in the jewelry department, where the French novelties loaded the trays and were displayed in the cases.

Nan forgot her friends—and the flight of time. It was not alone the pretty things displayed that interested her, but the wonderfully dressed women who paraded through the aisles of the store.

She found herself beside a beautifully dressed woman, in a loose, full-flowing fur garment, with fur hat to match, who, it seemed to Nan, was quite the most fashionable person she had ever beheld. The woman had a touch of rouge upon her otherwise pale cheeks; her eyebrows were suspiciously penciled; her lips were slightly ruddy. Nevertheless, she was very demure and very much the lady in appearance.

She was idly turning over lavalliéres on a tray—holding them up for inspection, and letting the pretty chains run through her fingers to drop into the tray again, like sparkling water.

"I don't think I care for any of these, don't you know?" she drawled, but very pleasantly. "I'm sorry—really."

She turned away from the counter. Nan was close by and had been secretly watching the pretty woman more than she had the lavalliéres. The clerk—rather an attractive girl with curly, black hair and very pink cheeks; quite an excitable young thing—suddenly leaned over the counter and whispered:

"Oh, madam! Pray! The special lavaliére I showed you is not here."

"What do you say, child?" demanded the woman, haughtily. "Do you miss anything?"

"The special lavaliére I showed you, madam," gasped the girl. "Forgive me—*do*! But I am responsible for all I take out of the case!"

"It is a mistake," said the woman, coldly. "I haven't the thing—surely."

"It is not here!" wailed the clerk, still in a low key, but fingering madly among the chains upon the tray. "Oh, ma'am! it will cost me twenty dollars!"

The woman turned slowly and her eyes—placid blue before—now shone with an angry light. Her gaze sought the counter—then the excited clerk—lastly, Nan!

"I haven't your lavaliére," she said, and although her voice was stern, it was low. "I haven't your lavaliére. How about this girl, here?" and she indicated Nan, with an air of superb indifference.

"Oh, madam!" gasped the clerk.

"Don't! don't!" begged Nan. "Oh! you *know* I haven't it!"

At that moment Nan felt a severe grasp upon her arm. She could not have run had she so desired. Her heart grew cold; her face flushed to fiery red. All neighboring eyes were turned on her.

In department stores like this the management finds it very unwise to make any disturbance over a case of loss or robbery. The store detective held on to Nan's arm; but he waited for developments.

"What is this all about, Miss Merwin?" he demanded of the clerk.

"I am charged with stealing a twenty-dollar lavaliére!" exclaimed the customer.

"Oh, impossible, madam!" said the detective, evidently recognizing her.

"Then this girl, who was nearest, may have it," said madam, sharply.

Nan was very much frightened; yet her sense of honesty came to her rescue. She cried:

"Why should I be accused? I am innocent—I assure you, I would not do such a thing. Why! I have more than twenty dollars in my purse right now. I will show you. Why should I steal what I can buy?"

To Nan Sherwood this question seemed unanswerable. But the store detective scarcely noticed. He looked at the lovely woman and asked:

"Madam is *sure* this girl took the lavalliére?"

"Oh, mercy, no! I would not accuse anybody of such a thing," responded the woman, in her low voice.

"But we know who you are, madam, we do not know this girl," said the detective, doubtfully. "You are a customer whom the store is glad to serve. This girl is quite unknown to us. I have no doubt but she is guilty—as you say."

He shook the troubled Nan by the arm. The girl was trying to control herself—to keep from breaking down and crying. Somehow, she felt that *that* would not help her in the least.

Without warning, a low voice spoke at Nan's side: "I know this girl. Of what is she accused?"

Only a few beside the detective and Nan heard the words.

"Of stealing something from the counter," said the man.

"I should not be surprised." The girl who had spoken, still whispered to the detective. "I know who she is. Her father is already in trouble on a similar charge. This girl tried to take a hand-bag of mine once. I never *did* think she was any better than she should be."

It was Linda Riggs. She stood with flushed face, looking at Nan, and although but few customers heard what she said, the latter felt as though she should sink through the floor.

"Ah-ha!" exclaimed the pompous detective, holding Nan's arm with a tighter grip. "You'll come with me to the superintendent's office to be searched."

Nothing but the vindictive expression of Linda's face kept Nan Sherwood from bursting into tears. She was both hurt and frightened by this situation. And to have her father's name mentioned in such an affair—perhaps printed in the papers! This thought terrified her as much as the possibility that she, herself, might be put in jail.

Rather unsophisticated about police proceedings was Nan, and she saw jail yawning for her just beyond the superintendent's office, whether the lost lavalliére was found in her possession or not.

But instantly, before the detective could remove the trembling girl from the spot, or many curious people gather to stare and comment upon the incident, the wonderfully dressed woman said to the detective in her careless drawl:

"Wait! Quite dramatic, I must say. So this other girl steps in and accuses our young heroine—without being asked even? I would doubt such testimony seriously, were I *you*, sir."

"But, madam!" exclaimed the man.

"*What* a situation—for the film!" pursued the woman, raising her lorgnette to look first at Nan and then at Linda Riggs. The latter was flushing and paling by turns—fearful at what she had done to her schoolmate, yet glad she had done it, too!

As the customer wheeled slowly in her stately way to view the railroad magnate's daughter, the clerk uttered a stifled cry, and on the heels of it the detective dropped Nan's arm to hop around the woman in great excitement.

"Wait, madam! wait, madam! wait!" he reiterated. "It is here—it is here!"

"What is the matter with you, pray?" asked the woman, curiously. "Have you taken leave of your senses? Why don't you stand still?"

"The lavalliére!" gasped the man and, reaching suddenly, he plucked the dangling chain from an entangling frog on her fur garment. "Here it is, madam!" he cried, with immense satisfaction.

"Now, fancy!" drawled the woman.

Linda slipped out of sight behind some other people. Nan felt faint—just as though she would drop. The clerk and the detective were lavish in their apologies to Nan. As for the woman whose garment had been the cause of all the trouble, she merely laughed.

"Fancy!" she said, in her low, pleasant drawl. "Just fancy! had I not chanced to be known to you, and a customer of the store, I might have been marched up to the superintendent's office myself. It really *is* a wonderfully good situation for a film—a real moving picture scene made to order."

CHAPTER XVIII

THE RUNAWAYS AGAIN

Nan was ordinarily brave enough. But the disgrace of this scene—in which the fashionably attired woman merely saw the dramatic possibilities—well nigh broke the girl's spirit. If she moved from this place she feared the whispering people would follow her; if she remained, they would remain to gape and wonder.

The troubled girl glanced hurriedly around. Was there no escape? Suppose her chum and Mrs. Mason and Grace should appear, searching for her?

The floodgates of her tears were all but raised when the placid woman who had caused all the trouble turned suddenly to her.

"I *do* owe an apology to you, my dear," she said. "I see you feel very badly about it. Don't. It really is not worth thinking of. You evidently have a spiteful enemy in that girl who has run away. But, of course, my dear, such unfounded accusations have no weight in the minds of sensible people." She seemed quite to have forgotten that hers was the first accusation.

She glanced about disdainfully upon the group of whispering women and girls. Some of them quite evidently recognized her. How could they help it, when her features were so frequently pictured on the screen? But Nan had not identified this woman with the great actress-director, whose films were being talked of from ocean to ocean.

"Come, my dear," she said. "We can find a quieter place to talk, I know. And I *do* wish to know you better."

Whether it were unwise or not, Nan Sherwood found it impossible to refuse the request of so beautiful a woman. Nan immediately fell under the charm of her beauty and her voice. She went with her dumbly and forgot the unpleasant people who stood about and stared. The lovely woman's light hand upon her arm, too, took away the memory of the detective's stern grasp.

The actress led her to the nearest elevator where a coin slipped into the palm of the elevator man caused him to shoot them up to another floor without delay. In this way all the curious ones lost trace of Nan and her new friend. In a few moments they were sitting in one of the tea-rooms where a white-aproned maid served them with tea and sweets at Madam's command.

"That is what you need, my dear," said Nan's host. "Our unfailing nerve-reviver and satisfier—tea. What would our sex do without it? And how do we manage to keep our complexions as we do, and still imbibe hogsheads of tea?"

She laughed and pinched Nan's cheek. "You have a splendid complexion yourself, child. And there's quite some film-charm in your features, I can see. Of course, you have never posed?"

"For moving pictures?" gasped Nan, at last waking up to what the woman meant. "Oh, no, indeed!"

"You are not like most other young girls, then?" said the woman. "You haven't the craze to act in the silent drama?"

"I never thought of such a thing," Nan innocently replied. "Film companies do not hire girls of my age, do they?"

"Not unless they are wonderfully well adapted for the work," agreed the actress. "But I am approached every week—I was going to say, every day—by girls no older than you, who think they have genius for the film-stage."

"Oh!" exclaimed Nan, beginning at last to take interest in something besides her recent unpleasant experience. "Do *you* make moving pictures?"

The actress raised her eyes and clasped her hands, invoking invisible spirits to hear. "At last! a girl who is not tainted by the universal craze for the movies—and who does not know *me*! There are still worlds for me to conquer," murmured the woman. "Yes, my child," she added, to the rather abashed Nan, "I am a maker of films."

"You—you must excuse me," Nan hastened to say. "I expect I ought to know all about you; but I lived quite a long time in the Michigan woods, and then, lately, I have been at boarding school, and we have no movies there."

"Your excuses are accepted, my dear," the actress-director said demurely. "It is refreshing, I assure you, to meet a girl like you."

"I—I suppose you see so many," Nan said eagerly. "Those looking for positions in your company, I mean. You do not remember them all?"

"Oh, mercy, no, my dear!" drawled the woman. "I see hundreds."

"Two girls I know of have recently come to Chicago looking for positions with moving picture concerns," explained Nan, earnestly. "They are country girls, and their folks want them to come home."

"Runaways?"

"Yes, ma'am. They have run away and their folks are dreadfully worried."

"I assure you," said the moving picture director, smiling, "they have not been engaged at my studio. New people must furnish references—especially if they chance to be under age. Two girls from the country, you say, my dear? How is it they have come to think they can act for the screen?" and she laughed lightly again.

Nan, sipping her tea and becoming more used to her surroundings and more confidential, told her new acquaintance all about Sallie Morton and Celia Snubbins.

"Dear, dear," the woman observed at last. "How can girls be so foolish? And the city is no place for them, alone, under any circumstances. If they should come to me I will communicate with their parents. I believe I should know them, my dear—two girls together, and both from the country?"

"Oh! if you only would help them," cried Nan. "I am sure such a kind act would be repaid."

The woman laughed. "I see you have faith in all the old fashioned virtues," she said. "Dear me, girl! I am glad I met you. Tell me how I may communicate with the parents of these missing girls?"

Nan did this; but she appreciated deeply the fact that the actress refrained from asking her any personal questions. After what Linda

Riggs had said at the jewelry counter, Nan shrank from telling her name or where she lived to anybody who had heard her enemy.

She parted from the moving picture director with great friendliness, however. As the latter kissed Nan she slipped a tiny engraved card into the girl's hand.

"Some time, when you have nothing better to do, my dear, come to see me," she said. It was not until Nan was by herself again that she learned from the card that she had been the guest of a very famous actress of the legitimate stage who had, as well, become notable as a maker of moving pictures.

The girl's heart was too sore at first, when she met her friends as agreed in an entirely different part of the great store, to say anything about her adventure. But that night, when she and Bess were alone, Nan showed her chum the famous actress' card, and told her how the moving picture director was likewise on the lookout for the two runaway girls.

"Splendid!" cried Bess. "Keep on and we'll have half the people in Chicago watching out for Sallie and Celia. But Nan! You do have the most marvelous way of meeting the most interesting people. Think of it! Knowing that very famous actress. How did you do it, Nan?"

"Oh! something happened that caused us to speak," Nan said lightly. But she winced at the thought of the unhappy nature of that incident. She was glad that Bess Harley was too sleepy to probe any deeper into the matter.

CHAPTER XIX

HOW THEY LOOKED ON THE SCREEN

Nan did not forget Inez, the flower-girl, nor the fact that the runaways—Sallie Morton and Celia Snubbins—might still be traced through Mother Beasley's cheap lodging house.

Both Walter and Grace Mason had been interested, as well as amused, in the chum's account of their first adventure in Chicago. The brother and sister who lived so far away from the squalor of Mother Beasley's and who knew nothing of the toil and shifts of the flower-seller's existence, were deeply moved by the recital of what Nan and Bess had observed.

"That poor little thing!" Grace said. "On the street in all weathers to sell posies—and for a drunken woman. Isn't it awful? Something should be done about it. I'll tell father."

"And he'd report the case to the Society," said her brother, promptly. "Father believes all charity should be done through organizations. 'Organized effort' is his hobby," added Walter, ruefully. "He says I lack proper appreciation of its value."

"But if he told the Society for the Prevention of Cruelty to Children about Inez, they would take her and put her in some institution," objected Nan.

"And put a uniform on her like a prisoner," cried Bess. "And make her obey rules like—like us boarding school girls. Oh, dear!"

The others laughed at that.

"Oh, you girls!" said Walter. "To hear you talk, one would think you were hounded like slaves at Lakeview Hall. You should have such a strict teacher as my tutor, for instance. He's the fellow for driving one. He says he'll have me ready for college in two years; but if he does, I know I shall feel as stuffed as a Strasburg goose."

"This learning so much that one will be glad to forget when one grows up," sighed Bess, "is an awful waste of time."

"Why, Bess!" cried Grace Mason, "don't you ever expect to read or write or spell or cipher when you grow up?"

"No more than I can help," declared the reckless Elizabeth.

"And yet you've always talked about our going to college together," said Nan, laughing at her chum.

"But college girls never have to use what they learn—except fudge-making and dancing, and—and—well, the things that aren't supposed to be in the curriculum," declared Bess.

"Treason! treason!" said Nan. "How dare you, Elizabeth? Pray what *do* girls go through college for?"

"To fit themselves for the marriage state," declared Bess. "My mother went to college and she says that every girl in her graduating class was married inside of five years—even the homely ones. You see, the homely ones make such perfectly splendid professors' wives. There's even a chance for Procrastination Boggs, you see."

"You ridiculous girl!" Nan said. "Come on! Who's going down town with me? I can find my way around now, for I have studied a map of Chicago and I can go by the most direct route to Mother Beasley's."

"And find that cunning little Inez, too?" asked Grace.

"Yes. If I want to. But to-day I want to go to see if Sallie and Celia went back to Mrs. Beasley's. I heard from Sallie's mother by this morning's post, and the poor woman is dreadfully worked up about the runaways. Mrs. Morton had a bad dream about Sallie, and the poor woman believes in dreams."

"She does!" exclaimed Grace. "I suppose she looks at a dream book every morning to see what each dream means. How funny!"

"Goodness!" cried Bess. "Come to think of it, I had the strangest dream last night. I dreamed that I saw myself in the looking-glass and my reflection stepped right out and began to talk to me. We sat down and talked. It was so funny—just as though I were twins."

"What an imagination!" exclaimed Walter. "You don't lack anything in that particular, for sure."

"Well," declared Bess, "I want to know what it means."

"I can make a pretty close guess," said Nan, shrewdly.

"'*Vell, vas ist?*' as our good Frau Deuseldorf says when she gets impatient with our slowness in acquiring her beloved German."

"It means," declared Nan, "that a combination of French pancake with peach marmalade, on top of chicken salad and mayonnaise, is not conducive to dreamless slumber. If you dreamt you met yourself on Grand Avenue parading at the head of a procession of Elizabeth Harleys, after such a dinner as you ate last night, I shouldn't be surprised."

"Carping critic!" exclaimed Bess, pouting. "*Do* let me eat what I like while I'm here. When we get back to Lakeview Hall you know Mrs. Cupp will want to put us all on half rations to counteract our holiday eating. I heard her bemoaning the fact to Dr. Beulah that we would come back with our stomachs so full that we would be unable to study for a fortnight."

"My! she is a Tartar, isn't she?" was Walter's comment.

"Oh, you don't know what we girls have to go through with at the Hall—what trials and privations," said his sister, feelingly.

"I can see it's making you thin, Sis," scoffed the boy. "And how about all those midnight suppers, and candy sprees, and the like?"

"Mercy!" exclaimed Bess. "If it were not for those extras we should all starve to death. There! we've missed that jitney. We'll have to wait for another."

The girls and their escort got safely to the shabby street in which Mother Beasley kept her eating and lodging house; but they obtained no new information regarding the runaway girls who had spent their first night in Chicago with the poor, but good-hearted widow.

Nor did they find Inez in her accustomed haunts near the railroad station; and it was too late that day to hunt the little flower-seller's lodging, for Inez lived in an entirely different part of the town.

"Rather a fruitless chase," Walter said, as they walked from the car on which they had returned. "What are you going to do about those runaway girls, now?"

"I don't know—oh! stop a moment!" Nan suddenly cried. "What's that over there?"

"A picture palace; goodness knows they're common enough," said Bess.

"But see what the sign says. Look, girls! Look, Walter!" and Nan excitedly pointed out the sheet hung above the arched entrance of the playhouse. "'A Rural Beauty'!" she cried. "That's the very picture those two girls took part in. It's been released."

"We must see it," Bess cried. "I'm just crazy to see how Sallie and Celia look on the screen."

"Why! you never saw them. Do you think they will be labeled?" scoffed Walter.

"Oh, we saw a photograph of Sallie; and if Celia looks anything like Mr. Si Snubbins, we can't mistake her," laughed Bess. "Let's run over and go in."

"No," Grace objected. "Mother never lets us go to a picture show without asking her permission first."

"No? Not even when Walter is with you?" asked Bess.

"No. She wishes to know just what kind of picture I am going to see. She belongs to a club that tries to make the picture-play people in this neighborhood show only nice films. She says they're not all to be trusted to do so."

"I guess this 'Rural Beauty' is a good enough picture," Nan said; "but of course we'll ask your mother's permission before we go in."

"There it is," groaned Bess. "Got to ask permission to breathe, I expect, pretty soon."

But she was glad, afterward, that they did ask Mrs. Mason. That careful lady telephoned the committee of her club having the censorship of picture plays in charge, and obtained its report upon "A Rural Beauty." Then she sent Walter to the playhouse to buy a block of seats for that evening, and over the telephone a dozen other boys and girls—friends of Grace and Walter—were invited to join the party.

They had a fine time, although the chums from Tillbury had not an opportunity of meeting all of the invited guests before the show.

"But they are all going home with us for supper—just like a grown-up theatre party," confided Grace to Nan and Bess.

"Pearl Graves telephoned that she would be a little late and would have to bring her cousin with her. Mother told her to come along, cousin and all, of course."

Nan and Bess, with a couple of friends of the Masons' whom they had already met, sat in the front row of the block of seats reserved for the party, and did not see the others when they entered the darkened house.

Several short reels were run off before the first scene of "A Rural Beauty" was shown. It was a very amusing picture, being full of country types and characters, with a sweet little love story that pleased the girls, and some quite adventurous happenings that made a hit with Walter, as he admitted.

Sallie Morton and Celia Snubbins were in the picture and the chums easily picked the runaways out on the screen. Sallie was a pretty girl, despite the fault her father had pointed out—that she was long-limbed. Nan and Bess knew Celia Snubbins because she *did* look like her father.

The two girls had been used in the comedy scene of "A Rural Beauty" as contrasts to the leading lady in the play, who was made up most strikingly as the beautiful milkmaid who captured the honest young farmer in the end.

There was a buzz of excitement among the Masons and those of their friends who had heard about the runaways over the appearance of Sallie and Celia when they came on the screen. As the party reached the lobby after the end of the last reel, Walter expressed his opinion emphatically regarding the runaway girls.

"I declare! I think those two girls awfully foolish to run away from home if they couldn't do anything more in a picture than they did in that one."

Nan was about to make some rejoinder, for Walter was walking beside her, when somebody said, back of them:

"Why, you must know those girls ahead. They go to Lakeview Hall with Gracie Mason."

"Goodness! they are not staying with Grace and Walter, are they?" demanded a shrill and well remembered voice. "Why, I saw Nan Sherwood in trouble in one of the big stores the other day, for taking something from one of the counters."

Nan turned, horrified. The speaker was Linda Riggs.

CHAPTER XX

NAN ON THE HEIGHTS

Mrs. Mason had not chaperoned the party of girls and boys to the motion picture show; but Miss Hagford, the English governess, was with them. Including the young hosts and Nan and Bess, there was almost a score in the party, and they made quite a bustling crowd in the lobby as they came out, adjusting their outer garments against the night air.

Walter and Nan were in the lead and when Linda Riggs' venomous tongue spat out the unkind words last repeated, few of the party heard her. Pearl Graves, her cousin, was beside the purse-proud girl who had been Nan's bitter enemy since the day they had first met. Pearl was a different kind of girl entirely from Linda; in fact, she did not know her cousin very well, for Linda did not reside in Chicago. At her cousin's harsh exclamation Pearl cried:

"Hush, Linda! how can you say such things? That can not possibly be true."

"'Tis, too! And Nan won't dare deny it," whispered Linda. "She knows what her father is, too! Mr. and Mrs. Mason can't have heard about Nan's father being in trouble for taking a man's watch and money in a sleeping car. Oh! *I* know all about it."

Walter Mason's ears were sharp enough; but Linda spoke so hurriedly, and the boy was so amazed, that the cruel girl got thus far in her wicked speech before he turned and vehemently stopped her.

"What do you mean by telling such a story as that about Nan?" demanded the boy, hoarsely. "And about her father, too? You are just the meanest girl I ever saw, Linda Riggs, and I'm sorry you're in this party. I wish you were a boy—I'd teach you one good lesson—I would!"

They stood just at the entrance to the theatre, where the electric lights were brightest. A few flakes of snow were falling, like glistening particles of tinsel. There were not many patrons entering the moving picture house at this late hour, but the remainder of the Masons' guests crowded forward to hear and see what was going on.

Nan was white-faced, but dry-eyed. Walter stood partly in front of her as though he were physically defending her, and held one of her hands while his other hand was tightly clenched, and his face ablaze with indignation.

"Oh, Nan! What is the matter?" cried Bess Harley, running to Nan's side and taking her other hand.

"What has happened?" asked Grace Mason. "What is it, Walter?"

"My goodness!" broke in Bess, before there could be any other explanation. "Here's that horrid Linda Riggs. What brought *her* here, I'd like to know?"

"I've as much right here as you have, Harley," cried Linda. "I don't have to worm myself into society that is above me, as you and your precious friend do. My father is as rich as any girl's father here, I'd have you know."

"Oh, hush, Linda!" murmured Pearl Graves, very much ashamed of her cousin.

"Walter! Grace! What does this mean?" demanded the governess, hurrying forward. "Don't make a scene here, I beg. Have no quarreling."

But Walter was too greatly enraged to be easily amenable to the mild lady's advice.

"What do you think of this, Miss Hagford?" he cried excitedly. "Nan Sherwood has been at our house since the first day she and Bess arrived in Chicago; yet Linda Riggs says she saw Nan taking something in a store here."

"Hush, Walter, hush!" begged Miss Hagford. "People will hear you."

"Well, people heard her!" declared the angry youth.

"We know Linda Riggs for what she is," Bess put in. "But these other boys and girls don't. Grace will tell you that Linda is the very meanest girl at Lakeview Hall."

"Oh! I couldn't say *that*, Bess," gasped timid Grace. "She is my guest for the evening!"

"Well, I'll say it for you," burst out her brother. "Somebody should tell the truth about her."

"So they should," chimed in Bess. "She's a mean, spiteful thing!"

"Stop! stop, all of you!" commanded the governess, sternly. "Why, this is disgraceful."

"I guess it is—I guess it is," said Linda, bitterly. "But this is the sort of treatment I might expect from anybody so much under the influence of Sherwood and Harley, as Grace and Walter are. I tell you I saw Nan Sherwood being held by a detective in Wilson-Meadows store, because they said she had taken some jewelry from the counter. And she cannot deny it!"

She said this with such positiveness, and was so much in earnest, that most of her hearers could not fail to be impressed. They stared at white-faced Nan to see if she had not something to say in her own defense. It seemed preposterous for Linda to repeat her charge so emphatically without some foundation for it.

"It isn't so!" cried Bess, first to gain her breath. "You know, Grace, Nan hasn't been shopping unless you and I were both with her. *That's* made up out of whole cloth!"

"You were not with her that day, Miss Smartie," cried the revengeful Linda. "And you see—she doesn't deny it."

"Of course she denies it!" Bess responded. "Do say something, Nan! Don't let that girl talk about you in this way."

Then Nan did open her lips—and what she said certainly amazed most of her hearers. "I was charged with taking a lavalliére from the counter. But it was found hanging from a lady's coat—"

"Where *you* hung it, when you saw you were caught!" interposed Linda.

"It was dreadful," Nan went on, brokenly. "I was so frightened and ashamed that I did not tell anybody about it."

"Nan!" cried Bess. "It's never *true*? You weren't arrested?"

"I—I should have been had the lavalliére not been found," her chum confessed. "Linda saw me and she told the man I was dishonest. I—I was so troubled by it all that I didn't tell anybody. It was the day I met that lady whose card I showed you, Bess. *She* was the lady whose coat caught up the chain. She was very kind to me."

"And Linda Riggs tried to make it worse for you, did she?" put in the indignant Walter.

"Hush, Walter!" commanded Miss Hagford. "We must have no more of this here. It is disgraceful. We will go directly home and your mother must know all the particulars. I don't know what she will say—I really do not," the troubled governess added.

"Oh, you can all go," snarled Linda. "You're welcome to the company of that Nan Sherwood. Pearl and I can find our way to her house. We'll leave you right now."

"Pearl is not going home, Linda," said her cousin. "You're not going to spoil all *my* fun for your own pleasure, I can tell you!"

"Stop, my dear," Miss Hagford said sternly. "Don't wrangle any more. Come! March! Walter, lead the way with your sister. Let us delay no longer."

Walter felt inclined to be obstinate and stick to Nan; but the latter slipped back with Bess, and they two walked arm in arm. Bess was frankly sobbing. They were tears of rage.

"Oh, dear! I wish I hadn't been brought up so respectably!" she gasped. "I wish I were like Inez. I'd slap that Linda Riggs' face and tear her hair out in big handfuls!"

Nan could not even smile at her chum's tearful emphasis. She felt very miserable indeed. She thought the English governess looked at her suspiciously. Some of the girls and boys must surely be impressed by what Linda had said. Had it been practical, Nan would have slipped out of the crowd and run away.

It was a rather silent party that passed through the snowy streets to the Mason house. Some of the girls and their escorts whispered together but this only added to the embarrassment of all concerned.

They reached the house at last. It was brightly lighted, for Mrs. Mason had promised to entertain royally. Her appearance at the door when it was opened, was quite in the nature of a surprise, however. She ran forward, her lovely gown trailing behind her and both hands outstretched.

"Where is our Nan?" she cried gaily. "Nan Sherwood! come here to me at once. You delightfully brave girl! And never to have talked about it!"

By this time she had the embarrassed Nan within the circle of her arms, and was smiling charmingly upon the others who trooped into the big entrance hall.

"What do you suppose she has done?" pursued Mrs. Mason, happily. "*You* must have known about it, Bess, for you were with Nan when she went to Lakeview Hall last September. Why, girls! this Nan of ours, when the train stopped at a station, went alone to the rescue of a child threatened by a rattlesnake, killed the snake, and rescued the child. What do you think of *that*?

"And now some of the passengers on that train, who saw the brave deed, have applied for and obtained a medal for bravery which has been brought here by a committee, and is to be presented to our Nan. You dear girl!" cried Mrs. Mason, kissing her heartily. "*What are you crying for?*"

CHAPTER XXI

LONG TO BE REMEMBERED

There were lights and music and flowers all about the big reception rooms, and a number of ladies and gentlemen were present besides the committee that had brought the medal for Nan. This was no time to retail such gossip as Linda Riggs had brought to her ears, and Miss Hagford, the governess, did not take her employer into her confidence at that time.

Besides, Nan was suddenly made the heroine of the hour.

If she had felt like running away as the party of young people returned to the Mason house from the moving picture show, Nan was more than desirous of escape now. The situation was doubly embarrassing after Linda Riggs' cruel accusation; for Nan had the feeling that some, at least, of these strange girls and boys must believe Linda's words true.

Nan knew that, all the way from the picture show, Linda had been eagerly giving her version of the difficulties that had risen between them since she and Nan had first met on the train going to Lakeview Hall. These incidents are fully detailed in the previous volume of this series, "Nan Sherwood at Lakeview Hall," as likewise is the incident which resulted in the presentation to Nan of the medal for bravery.

The ladies and gentlemen who had made it their business to obtain this recognition of a very courageous act, had traced the modest schoolgirl by the aid of Mr. Carter, the conductor of the train on which Nan and Bess had been so recently snow-bound.

The committee were very thoughtful. They saw that the girl was greatly embarrassed, and the presentation speech was made very brief. But Mrs. Mason, with overflowing kindness, had arranged for a gala occasion. A long table was set in the big dining room, and the grown folk as well as the young people gathered around the board.

The ill-breeding of Linda Riggs, and her attempt to hurt Nan's reputation in the eyes of the Masons' friends, were both smothered under the general jollity and good feeling. Afterward Bess Harley declared that Linda must have fairly "stewed in her own venom." Nobody paid any attention to Linda, her own cousin scarcely speaking to her. Only once did the railroad magnate's daughter have an opportunity of showing her ill-nature verbally.

This was when the beautiful gold medal was being passed around the table for the inspection of the company individually. It came in the course of events, to Linda. She took the medal carelessly and turned it over on her palm.

"Oh, indeed—very pretty, I am sure. And, of course, useful," she murmured. "I have been told that most of these medals finally find their way to the pawnshops."

This speech made Mrs. Mason, who heard it, look curiously at Linda; the girls about her were silent—indeed, nobody made any rejoinder. It caused Mrs. Mason, however, to make some inquiries of Miss Hagford, and later of Grace and Bess.

The young folk danced for an hour to the music of a big disc machine. The committee of presentation had bidden Nan good-bye, and thanked Mrs. Mason for her hospitality. The party was breaking up.

Mrs. Mason called the young people together when the wraps of those who were leaving were already on.

"One last word, boys and girls, before we separate," the lady said softly, her arm around Nan, by whom she seemed to stand quite by chance. "I hope you have all had a pleasant time. If we cultivate a happy spirit we will always find pleasure wherever we go. Remember that.

"Criticism and back-biting in any social gathering breed unhappiness and discontent. And we should all be particularly careful how we speak of or to one another. I understand that there was one incident to mar this otherwise perfect evening. One girl was unkind enough to try to hurt the feelings of another by a statement of unmistakable falsehood."

Mrs. Mason's voice suddenly became stern. She was careful to avert her gaze from Linda Riggs' direction; but they all knew to whom she referred.

"I speak of this, boys and girls, for a single reason," the lady pursued. "For fear some of you may go home with any idea in your minds that the accusation against the girl vilified or against her father is in any particular true, I want you to tell your parents that *I* stand sponsor for both our dear Nan and her father. Neither could be guilty of taking that which was not his.

"Now, good-night all! I hope you have had a lovely time. I am sure this night will long be remembered by our Nan!"

The boys, led by Walter, broke into a hearty cheer for Nan Sherwood. Every girl save Linda came to kiss her good-night. Her triumph seemed unalloyed.

Yet the first mail in the morning brought a letter which dealt a staggering blow to Nan's Castle of Delight. Her mother wrote in haste to say that Mr. Ravell Bulson had been to the automobile manufacturers with whom Mr. Sherwood had a tentative contract, and had threatened to sue Mr. Sherwood if he did not return to him, Bulson, his lost watch and chain and roll of bankbills, amounting to several hundred dollars.

The automobile manufacturers had served notice on Mr. Sherwood that they would delay the signing of any final contract until Bulson's accusation was refuted. Almost all of Mrs. Sherwood's ready money, received through the Scotch courts, had been invested in the new automobile showroom and garage.

CHAPTER XXII

WHAT HAS BECOME OF INEZ?

Nan could not bring herself to speak of the sudden turn her father's difficulties had taken. She had long-since learned that family affairs were not to be discussed out of the family circle.

It was bad enough, so she thought, to have Tillbury and Owneyville people discussing the accusation of Ravell Bulson, without telling all the trouble to her friends here in Chicago. Enough had been said on the previous evening, Nan thought, about the matter. She hid this new phase of it even from her chum.

It was Bess who suggested their activities for this day. She wanted to do something for Inez, the flower-girl, in whom usually thoughtless Bess had taken a great interest. She had written to her mother at once about the poor little street arab, and Mrs. Harley had sent by express a great bundle of cast-off dresses outgrown by Bess' younger sisters, that easily could be made to fit Inez.

Mrs. Mason had shoes and stockings and hats that might help in the fitting out of the flower-seller; and she suggested that the child be brought to the house that her own sewing maid might make such changes in the garments as would be necessary to make them of use for Inez.

"Not that the poor little thing is at all particular, I suppose, about her clothes," Bess remarked. "I don't imagine she ever wore a garment that really fitted her, or was made for her. Her shoes weren't mates — I saw that the other day, didn't you, Nan?"

"I saw that they were broken," Nan agreed, with a sigh. "Poor little thing!"

"And although fashion allows all kinds of hats this season, I am very sure that straw of hers had seen hard service for twelve months or more," Bess added.

Walter, hearing the number and street of Inez's lodging, insisted upon accompanying the chums on their errand. Grace did not go.

She frankly admitted that such squalid places as Mother Beasley's were insufferable; and where Inez lived might be worse.

"I'm just as sorry for such people as I can be and I'd like to help them all," Grace said. "But it makes me actually ill to go near them. How mother can delve as she does in the very slums—well, I can't do it! Walter is like mother; he doesn't mind."

"I guess you're like your father," said Bess. "He believes in putting poor people into jails, otherwise institutions, instead of giving them a chance to make good where they are. And there aren't enough institutions for them all. I never supposed there were so many poor people in this whole world as we have seen in Chicago.

"I used to just detest the word 'poor'—Nan'll tell you," confessed Bess. "I guess being with Nan has kind of awakened me to 'our duties,' as Mrs. Cupp would say," and she laughed.

"Oh!" cried Grace. "I'd do for them, if I could. But I don't even know how to talk to them. Sick babies make me feel so sorry I want to cry, and old women who smell of gin and want to sell iron-holders really scare me. Oh, dear! I guess I'm an awful coward!"

Nan laughed. "What are you going to do with that crisp dollar bill I saw your father tuck into your hand at breakfast, Gracie?" she asked.

"Oh, I don't know. I hadn't thought. Papa is always so thoughtful. He knows I just *can't* make ends meet on my fortnightly allowance."

"But you don't absolutely need the dollar?"

"No-o."

"Then give it to us. We'll spend it for something nice with which to treat those kid cousins that Inez told us about."

"Good idea," announced Walter. "It won't hurt you to give it to charity, Sis."

"All right," sighed Grace. "If you really all say so. But there is such a pretty tie down the street at Libby's."

"And you've a million ties, more or less," declared Bess. "Of course we'll take it from her, Walter. Come on, now! I'm ready."

Under Walter's piloting the chums reached the street and number Inez had given Nan. It was a cheap and dirty tenement house. A woman told them to go up one flight and knock on the first door at the rear on that landing.

They did this, Walter insisting upon keeping near the girls. A red-faced, bare-armed woman, blowsy and smelling strongly of soapsuds, came to the door and jerked it open.

"Well?" she demanded, in a loud voice.

Bess was immediately tongue-tied; so Nan asked:

"Is Inez at home?"

"And who be you that wants Inez—the little bothersome tyke that she is?"

"We are two of her friends," Nan explained briefly. It was plain that the woman was not in a good temper, and Nan was quite sure she had been drinking.

"And plenty of fine friends she has," broke out the woman, complainingly. "While I'm that poor and overrun with children, that I kin scarce get bite nor sup for 'em. And she'll go and spend her money on cakes and ice-cream because it's my Mamie's birthday, instead of bringing it all home, as I told her she should! The little tyke! I'll l'arn her!"

"I am sorry if Inez has disobeyed you," said Nan, breaking in on what seemed to promise to be an unending complaint. "Isn't she here—or can you tell us where to find her?"

"I'll say 'no' to them two questions immediate!" exclaimed the woman, crossly. "I beat her as she deserved, and took away the money she had saved back to buy more flowers with; and I put her basket in the stove."

"Oh!" gasped Bess.

"And what is it to *you*, Miss?" demanded the woman, threateningly.

"It was cruel to beat her," declared Bess, bravely, but unwisely.

"Is that so? is that so?" cried the virago, advancing on Bess with the evident purpose of using her broad, parboiled palm on the visitor, just as she would use it on one of her own children. "I'll l'arn ye not to come here with your impudence!"

But Walter stepped in her way, covering Bess' frightened retreat. Walter was a good-sized boy.

"Hold on," he said, good-naturedly. "We won't quarrel about it. Just tell us where the child is to be found."

"I ain't seen her for four days and nights, that I haven't," declared the woman.

That was all there was to be got out of her. Nan and her friends went away, much troubled. They went again to Mother Beasley's to inquire, with like result. When they told that kind but careworn woman what the child's aunt had said, she shook her head and spoke lugubriously.

"She was probably drunk when she treated the child so. If she destroyed Inez basket and used the money Inez always saved back to buy a new supply of bouquets, she fair put the poor thing out o' business."

"Oh, dear!" said Nan. "And we can't find her on the square."

"Poor thing! I wisht she had come here for a bite—I do. I'd have trusted her for a meal of vittles."

"I am sure you would, Mrs. Beasley," Nan said, and she and her friends went away very much worried over the disappearance of Inez, the flower-seller.

CHAPTER XXIII

JUST TOO LATE

Walter Mason was not only an accommodating escort; he was very much interested in the search for Inez. Even Bess, who seldom admitted the necessity for boys at any time in her scheme of life, admitted on this occasion that she was glad Walter was present.

"That woman, poor little Inez's aunt, would have slapped my face, I guess," she admitted. "Isn't it mean of her to speak so of the child? And she had beaten her! I don't see how you had the courage to face her, Walter."

"I should give him my medal," chuckled Nan. "Where now, Walter?"

"To see that officer," declared the boy.

The trio were again on the square where Inez had told Nan she almost always sold her flowers. Walter came back in a few moments from his interview with the police officer.

"Nothing doing," he reported. "The man says he hasn't seen her for several days, and she was always here."

"I suppose he knows whom we mean?" worried Bess.

"Couldn't be any mistake about that," Walter said. "He is afraid she is sick."

"I'm not," Nan said promptly. "It is just as Mrs. Beasley says. If her aunt took Inez's basket and money away, she is out of business. She's lost her capital. I only hope she is not hungry, poor thing."

"Dear, dear!" joined in Bess. "If she only knew how to come to us! She must know we'd help her."

"She knows where we are staying," Nan said. "Don't you remember I showed her Walter's card?"

"Then why hasn't she been to see us?" cried Bess.

"I guess there are several reasons for that," said sensible Nan.

"Well! I'd like to know what they are," cried her chum. "Surely, she could find her way."

"Oh, yes. Perhaps she didn't want to come. Perhaps she is too proud to beg of us—just beg *money*, I mean. She is an independent little thing."

"Oh, I know that," admitted Bess.

"But more than likely," Nan pursued, "her reason for not trying to see us was that she was afraid she would not be admitted to the house."

"My gracious!" exclaimed Walter. "I never thought of that."

"Just consider what would happen to a ragged and dirty little child who mounted your steps—even suppose she got that far," Nan said.

"What would happen to her?" demanded the wondering Bess, while Walter looked thoughtful.

"If she got into the street at all (there is always a policeman on fixed post at the corner) one of the men at the house, the butler or the footman, would drive her away.

"You notice that beggars never come through that street. They are a nuisance and wealthy people don't want to see people in rags about their doorsteps. Even the most charitable people are that way, I guess," added Nan.

"Your mother is so generous, Walter, that if beggars had free access to the street and the house, she could never go out of an afternoon without having to push her way through a throng of the poor and diseased to reach her carriage."

"Oh, mercy!" cried Bess.

"I guess that is so," admitted Walter. "You've got mother sized up about right."

"I know it's so," said Nan, quickly. "Do you know, I think your mother, Walter, would have made a good chatelaine of a castle in medieval times. Then charitably inclined ladies were besieged by the poor and miserable at their castle gates. The good lady gave them largess as she stepped into her chariot. Their servants threw silver pennies at a distance so that the unfortunates would scramble for the coins and leave a free passage for miladi.

"In those days," pursued Nan, quite in earnest, "great plagues used to destroy a large portion of the population—sweeping through the castles of the rich as well as the hovels of the poor. That was because the beggars hung so upon the skirts of the rich. Wealth paid for its cruelty to poverty in those days, by suffering epidemics of disease with the poor."

"Goodness, Nan! I never thought of that," said Walter. "What a girl you are."

"She reads everything," said Bess, proudly; "even statistics."

Nan laughed heartily. "I did not get *that* out of a book of statistics, Bess. But that is why we have so many hospitals and institutions for housing poor and ill people. Society has had to make these provisions for the poor, to protect itself."

"Now you sound like a regular socialist or anarchist or something," said Bess, somewhat vaguely.

"You'd have heard it all before, if you'd listened to some of Dr. Beulah's lectures in the classroom," Nan said. "But we're far off the subject of Inez. I wish we could find her; but there seems no way."

"Oh, Nan! are you sure? Put on your thinking-cap," begged Bess.

"I have thought," her chum replied. "I thought of trying to trace her through the people who sell flowers to her. I asked Mrs. Beasley, and she told me that the flowers Inez sells come from the hotels and big restaurants where they have been on the tables over night. They are sorted and sold cheap to street pedlers like Inez. Hundreds of little ragamuffins buy and hawk these bouquets about the streets. The men who handle the trade would not be likely to remember one little girl.

"Besides," added Nan, smiling sadly. "Inez is a bankrupt. She is out of business altogether. The few pennies she saved back every day—rain or shine, whether she went hungry, or was fed—was her capital; and that her aunt took away. I'm dreadfully worried about the poor thing," concluded Nan, with moist eyes.

She felt so bad about it that she could not bring herself to join the matinée party that had been arranged by Grace for that afternoon. Some of the girls were going to have a box at a musical comedy, with Miss Hagford as chaperon.

Nan did not plead a headache; indeed, she was not given to white lies. She wished to call on the lovely actress whom she had met the day of her adventure in the department store. She wanted to inquire if she had seen or heard anything of the runaways, Sallie and Celia.

"I'd dearly love to go with you," Bess observed. "Just think of your knowing such a famous woman. You have all the luck, Nan Sherwood."

"I'm not sure that it was *good* fortune that brought me in contact with the lady," Nan returned ruefully.

"Well! it turned out all right, at least," said Bess. "And *my* escapades never do. I never have any luck. If it rained soup and I was hungry, you know I wouldn't have any spoon."

Nan set forth before the other girls started for the theatre. She knew just how to find the fashionable apartment hotel in which the actress lived, for she and her friends had passed it more than once in the car.

At the desk the clerk telephoned up to the actress' apartment to see if she was in, and would receive Nan. The maid did not understand who Nan was, and was doubtful; but the moment Madam came to the telephone herself and heard Nan's name, she cried:

"Send her up—send her up! She is just the one I want to see."

This greatly excited Nan, for she thought of Sallie and Celia. When she was let out of the elevator on one of the upper floors, the apartment door was open, and Madam herself was holding out a welcoming hand to her, excitedly saying:

"You dear girl! You are as welcome as the flowers in May. Come in and let me talk to you. How surprising, really! I had no thought of seeing you, and yet I desired to—so much."

Nan was drawn gently into the large and beautiful reception room, while the actress was talking. She saw the woman's furs and hat thrown carelessly on a couch, and thought that she must have recently come in, even before Madam said:

"I have just come from an exhausting morning in the studio. Oh, dear! everybody seemed so stupid to-day. There are such days, you know—everything goes wrong, and even the patient camera-man loses his temper.

"Yes, Marie, you may bring the tea tray. I am exhausted; nothing but tea will revive this fainting pilgrim.

"And, my dear!" she added, turning to Nan again, "I have news for you—news of those runaway girls."

"Oh, Madam! Are Sallie and Celia found?" cried Nan. "I want so to make Mrs. Morton happy."

"We-ell," said the actress, with less enthusiasm. "I believe I can give you a trace of them. But, of course, I haven't them shut up in a cage waiting for their parents to come for them," and she laughed.

"It really is an odd occurrence, my dear. At the time I was telling you the other day that those girls could not be working with my company, that is exactly what they were doing."

"Oh!" cried Nan, again.

"Yes, my dear. Just fancy! I only learned of it this very morning. Of course, I give no attention to the extra people, save when they are before the camera. My assistant hires them and usually trains the 'mob' until I want them.

"Now, fancy!" pursued the lovely woman, "there was a girl, named Jennie Albert, whom we had been using quite a good deal, and she fell ill. So she sent two new girls, and as Mr. Gray needed two extras that day, he let them stay without inquiring too closely into their personal affairs.

"Oh, I blame Mr. Gray, and I told him so. I did not see the girls in question until the big scene we put on this morning. Then the company before the camera was too large; the scene was crowded. I began weeding out the awkward ones, as I always do.

"Why, positively, my dear, there are some girls who do not know how to wear a frock, and yet they wish to appear in *my* films!

"These two girls of whom I speak I cut out at once. I told Mr. Gray never to put them into costume again. Why! sticks and stones have more grace of movement and naturalness than those two poor creatures—positively!" cried the moving picture director, with emphasis.

"Ah, well! I must not excite myself. This is my time for relaxation, and—a second cup of tea!"

Her light laughter jarred a bit on Nan Sherwood's troubled mind.

"To think!" the lovely actress said, continuing, "that it never occurred to my mind that those two awkward misses might be your runaways until I was standing on one side watching the scene as they passed out. One was crying. Of course I am sorry I had to order their discharge, but one must sacrifice much for art," sighed Madam.

"One was crying, and I heard the other call her 'Celia.' And then the crying girl said: 'I can't help it, Sallie. I am discouraged'—or something like that.

"Of course, you understand, my dear, my mind was engaged with far more important matters. My sub-consciousness must have filmed the words, and especially the girls' names. After the scene suited me, it suddenly came back to me that those names were the *real* names of the runaway girls. They had given Mr. Gray fictitious names, of course. When I sent him out to find them, he was just too late. The girls had left the premises."

CHAPTER XXIV

OTHER PEOPLE'S WORRIES

Nan had written home quite fully about the presentation of the medal. It was the first her father and mother had known of the courage she had displayed so many weeks before in saving the life of the tiny girl at the Junction.

The fact that some of her fellow passengers had seen the act and considered it worthy of commemoration, of course, pleased Mr. and Mrs. Sherwood; but that Nan had been in peril herself on the occasion, naturally worried her mother.

"I hope you will not go about seeking other adventures, my dear child," wrote her mother, with gentle raillery. "What with your announcement of the presentation of the medal, and Mrs. Mason's enthusiastic letter, your father and I begin to believe that we have a kind of female knight errant for a daughter. I am afraid we never shall get our little Nan back again."

Nan did not really need any bubble of self-importance pricked in this way. She was humbly thankful to have been able to save the little girl from the snake, and that the horrid creature had not harmed her, either.

She had hidden the medal away, and would not display it or talk about it. The thought that her name and her exploit were on the Roll of Honor of the National Society actually made Nan's ears burn.

She had other worries during these brief winter days—mostly other people's worries, however. The absolute disappearance of Inez was one; another was the whereabouts of the two runaway girls, Sallie and Celia, who should by this time have discovered that they were not destined to be great motion picture actresses.

Nan had come away from the apartment of her friend, "the Moving Picture Queen," as Walter called her, that afternoon, with the address of the studio and a letter to Madam's assistant, Mr. Gray. The next morning, she and Bess went to the studio to make inquiries about the runaway girls. They went alone because Grace had much to do before returning to school; and now their day of departure for Lakeview was close at hand.

"And oh! how I hate to go back to those horrid studies again," groaned Bess.

Nan laughed. "What a ridiculous girl you are, Bess Harley," she said. "You were just crazy to go to Lakeview in the first place."

"Yes! wasn't I?" interposed Bess, gloomily. "But I didn't know I was crazy."

When once the chums came to the motion picture studio they had no thought for anything but their errand and the interesting things they saw on every side. At a high grilled gate a man let them into the courtyard after a glance at the outside of the letter Nan carried.

"You'll find Mr. Gray inside somewhere," said the gatekeeper. "You'll have to look for him."

Nan and Bess were timid, and they hesitated for some moments in the paved yard, uncertain which of the several doors to enter. They saw a number of girls and men enter through the gate as they had, and watched the men hurry to one door, and the women and girls to another.

"Lets follow those girls," suggested Bess, as a chattering trio went into the building. "We can't go far wrong, for the sheep and the goats seem to be separated," and she giggled.

"Meaning the men from the women?" said Nan. "I guess those doors lead to the dressing rooms."

She was right in this, for when the two friends stepped doubtfully into a long, high, white-plastered passage, which was quite empty, but out of which many doors opened, they heard a confusion of conversation and laughter from somewhere near.

"What are you going to do?" asked Bess, at once—and as usual—shifting all responsibility to her chum's shoulders. "Knock at all the doors, one after the other, until we find somebody who will direct us further?"

"Maybe that would not be a bad idea, Bess," Nan returned. "But—"

Just then a door opened and the confusion of voices burst on the visitors' ears with startling directness. A girl, dressed as a Gypsy, gaudy of raiment and bejeweled with brilliantly colored glass beads, almost ran the chums down as she tried to pull the door to behind her. The girl's face was painted with heavy shadows and much white, and so oddly that it looked almost like the make-up for a clown's part.

"Hello, kids. Going in here?" she asked pleasantly enough, refraining from closing the door entirely.

Nan and Bess obtained a good view of the noisy room. It was lighted by high windows and a skylight. There were rows of lockers for the girls' clothes along the blank wall of the room. Through the middle and along the sides were long tables and stools. The tables were divided into sections, each of which had its own make-up and toilet outfit.

A mature woman was going about, re-touching many of the girl's faces and scolding them, as Nan and Bess could hear, for not putting on the grease paint thick enough.

"That nasty stuff!" gasped Bess, in Nan's ear. "I wouldn't want to put it on my face."

Right then and there Bess lost all her desire for posing for the moving picture screen. Nan paid little attention to her, but ran after the girl who was hurrying through the passage toward the rear of the great building.

"Oh, wait, please!" cried Nan. "I want to find Mr. Gray—and I know he can't be in that dressing-room."

"Gray? I should say not," and the girl in costume laughed. Then she saw the letter in Nan's hand. "Is that for Gray?"

"Yes," Nan replied.

"Come along then. I expect he's been waiting for me for half an hour now—and believe me, he's just as kind and considerate as a wild bull when we keep him waiting. I overslept this morning."

It was then after ten o'clock, and Nan wondered how one could "oversleep" so late.

"I'm only glad Madam isn't going to be here this morning. By the way," the girl added, curiously, "who's your letter from? You and your friend trying to break into the movies?"

"My goodness, no!" gasped Nan. "I have no desire to act—and I'm sure I have no ability."

"It might be fun," Bess said doubtfully. "But do you all have to paint up so awfully?"

"Yes. That's so we will look right on the screen. Here! that's Gray—the bald-headed man in the brown suit. I hope you have better luck than two girls from the country who were in here for a couple of days. Gray bounced them yesterday. Who's your letter from?" added the girl, evidently disbelieving what both Nan and Bess had said when they denied having any desire to pose for the screen.

"Madam, herself," said Nan, demurely. "Do you think Mr. Gray will give me a hearing?"

"Well, I guess yes," cried the girl in costume. "Oh, do give it to him just as he starts in laying me out, will you?"

"Anything to oblige," Nan said, smiling. "Can we go right over and speak to him?"

"After me," whispered the girl. "Don't get into any of the 'sets,' or you'll get a call-down, too."

They had entered an enormous room, half circular in shape, with the roof and the "flat" side mostly glass. There were countless screens to graduate the light, and that light was all directed toward the several small, slightly raised stages, built in rotation along the curved wall of the studio.

Each of these stages had its own "set" of scenery and was arranged for scenes. On two, action of scenes was taking place while the energetic directors were endeavoring to get out of their people the pantomimic representation of the scenario each had in charge.

One director suddenly clapped his hands and shouted.

"Get this, John! All ready! You dude and cowboy start that scene now. Be sure you run on at the right cue, Miss Legget. Now, John! Ready boys?"

The representation of a tussle between a cowboy and an exquisitely dressed Eastern youth, in which comedy bit the so-called dude disarmed the Westerner and drove him into a corner till his sweetheart bursts in to protect him from the "wild Easterner," went to a glorious finish.

The camera clicked steadily, the man working it occasionally calling out the number of feet of blank film left on the spool so that the director might know whether to hasten or retard the action of the picture.

Nan and Bess stopped, as they were warned by the girl dressed in Gypsy costume, and watched the proceedings eagerly. Just as the scene came to an end the bald man in the brown suit strode over to the three girls.

"What do you mean by keeping me waiting, Miss Penny?" he demanded in a tone that made Bess shrink away and tremble. "Your scene has been set an hour. I want—Humph! what do *these* girls want? Did you bring them in?"

Miss Penny poked Nan sharply in the ribs with her elbow. "Show him the letter," she whispered. Adding aloud: "Oh, I brought them in, Mr. Gray. That's what delayed me. When I saw they had a letter for you—"

"For me?" snorted the director, and took doubtfully enough the epistle Nan held out to him. But when he sighted the superscription he tore it open with an exclamation of impatient surprise.

"*Now*, what does Madam want?" he muttered, and those few words revealed to Nan Sherwood what she had suspected to be the fact about the director—that she was a very exacting task-mistress.

Miss Penny, nodding slily to Nan and Bess, slipped away to the stage on which the Gypsy camp was set, and around which several men in brigandish looking costumes were lounging.

"What's this you young ladies want of me?" asked the director, rather puzzled, it seemed, after reading the note. "All she writes is to recommend Miss Sherwood to my attention and then includes a lot of instructions for to-morrow's work." He smiled sourly. "She is not explicit. Do you want work?"

"Oh, mercy me! no!" cried Nan.

"I should say not!" murmured Bess.

The director's worried, querulous face showed relief. He listened attentively while Nan explained about the runaways. She likewise repeated the actress' version of the discharging of the girls whom she had afterward identified as the two for whom Nan and Bess were in search.

"Yes, yes! I remember. And Madam was quite right in that instance," grudgingly admitted the director. He drew a notebook from his pocket and fluttered the leaves. "Yes. Here are their names crossed off my list. 'Lola Montague' and 'Marie Fortesque.' I fancy," said Mr. Gray, chuckling, "they expected to see those names on the bills."

"But, oh, Mr. Gray!" cried Nan Sherwood, feeling in no mood for laughing at silly Sallie Morton and Celia Snubbins. "Don't you know where they live—those two poor girls?"

"Why—no. They were extras and we get plenty of such people," said the director, carelessly. "Now, the girl who sent them is as daring a girl as I ever saw. I'm sorry she's hurt, or sick, or something, for although Jenny Albert has little 'film charm,' as we call it, she is useful—

"There!" suddenly broke off Mr. Gray. "You might try Jenny's address. She sent those girls here. She probably knows where they live."

He hastily wrote down the street and number on a card and handed it to Nan. "Sorry. That's the best I can do for you, Miss Sherwood."

He turned away, taking up his own particular worries again.

"And, goodness me, Nan!" sighed Bess, as they went out of the cluttered studio, back through the passage, and so into the courtyard and the street again. "Goodness me! I think *we* have the greatest lot of other people's worries on our shoulders that I ever heard of. We seem to collect other folk's troubles. How do we manage it?"

CHAPTER XXV

RUNAWAYS OF A DIFFERENT KIND

The chums, on leaving the moving picture studio, stopped to read more carefully the card Mr. Gray, the director, had given them. The street on which Jennie Albert lived was quite unknown to Nan and Bess and they did not know how to find it.

Besides, Nan remembered that Mrs. Mason trusted her to go to the moving picture studio, and to return without venturing into any strange part of the town.

"Of course," groaned Bess, "we shall have to go back and ask her."

"Walter will find the place for us," Nan said cheerfully.

"Oh—Walter! I hate to depend so on a boy."

"You're a ridiculous girl," laughed her chum. "What does it matter *whom* we depend upon? We must have somebody's help in every little thing in this world, I guess."

"Our sex depends too much upon the other sex," repeated Elizabeth, primly, but with dancing eyes.

"Votes for Women!" chuckled Nan. "You are ripe for the suffragist platform, Bessie. I listened to that friend of Mrs. Mason's talking the other day, too. She is a lovely lady, and I believe the world will be better—in time—if women vote. It is growing better, anyway.

"She told a funny story about a dear old lady who was quite converted to the cause until she learned that to obtain the right to vote in the first place, women must depend upon the men to give it to them. So, to be consistent, the old lady said she must refuse to accept _any_thing at the hands of the other sex—the vote included!"

"There!" cried Bess, suddenly. "Talk about angels—"

"And you hear their sleighbells," finished Nan. "Hi, Walter! Hi!"

They had come out upon the boulevard, and approaching along the snow-covered driveway was Walter Mason's spirited black horse and Walter driving in his roomy cutter.

The horse was a pacer and he came up the drive with that rolling action peculiar to his kind, but which takes one over the road very rapidly. A white fleck of foam spotted the pacer's shiny chest. He was sleek and handsome, but with his rolling, unblinded eyes and his red nostrils, he looked ready to bolt at any moment.

Walter, however, had never had an accident with Prince and had been familiar with the horse from the time it was broken to harness. Mr. Mason was quite proud of his son's horsemanship.

Walter saw Nan as she leaped over the windrow of heaped up snow into the roadway, and with a word brought Prince to a stop without going far beyond the two girls. There he circled about and came back to the side of the driveway where Nan and Bess awaited him.

"Hop in, girls. There's room for two more, all right," cried Walter. "I'll sit between you. One get in one side—the other on t'other. 'Round here, Nan—that's it! Now pull the robe up and tuck it in—sit on it. Prince wants to travel to-day. We'll have a nice ride."

"Oh-o-o!" gasped Bess, as they started. "Not too fast, Walter."

"I won't throw the clutch into high-gear," promised Walter, laughing. "Look out for the flying ice, girls. I haven't the screen up, for I want to see what we're about."

Walter wore automobile goggles, and sat on the edge of the seat between the two girls, with his elbows free and feet braced. If another sleigh whizzed past, going in the same direction, Prince's ears went back and he tugged at the bit. He did not like to be passed on the speedway.

Bess quickly lost her timidity—as she always did—and the ride was most enjoyable. When the first exuberance of Prince's spirit had worn off, and he was going along more quietly, the girls told Walter what they had seen and heard at the motion picture studio.

"Great luck!" pronounced the boy. "I'd like to get into one of those places and see 'em make pictures. I've seen 'em on the street; but that's different. It must be great."

"But we didn't find Sallie and Celia there," complained Nan.

"You didn't expect to, did you?" returned the boy. "But I know where that street is. We'll go around there after lunch if mother says we may, and look for that girl who knows them."

"Oh, Bess!"

"Oh, Nan!"

The chums had caught sight of the same thing at the same moment. Just ahead was a heavy sleigh, with plumes on the corner-posts, drawn by two big horses. They could not mistake the turnout. It belonged to the Graves' family with whom Linda Riggs was staying.

The chums had not seen Linda since the evening of the party, when the railroad president's daughter had acted in such an unladylike manner.

"I see the big pung," laughed Walter. "And I bet Linda's in it, all alone in her glory. Pearl told me she hated the thing; but that her grandmother considers it the only winter equipage fit to ride in. You ought to see the old chariot they go out in in summer.

"Hello," he added. "Got to pull up here."

A policeman on horseback had suddenly ridden into the middle of the driveway. Just ahead there was a crossing and along the side road came clanging a hospital ambulance, evidently on an emergency call.

The white-painted truck skidded around the corner, the doctor on the rear step, in his summerish looking white ducks, swinging far out to balance the weight of the car.

The pair of horses drawing the Graves' sleigh, snorted, pulled aside and rose, pawing, on their hind legs. The coachman had not been ready for such a move and he was pitched out on his head.

The girls and Walter heard a shrill scream of terror. The footman left the sleigh in a hurry, too—jumping in a panic. Off the two frightened horses dashed—not up the boulevard, but along the side street.

"That's Linda," gasped Bess.

"And she's alone," added Nan.

"Say! she's going to get all the grandeur she wants in a minute," exclaimed Walter. "Why didn't she jump, too, when she had the chance?"

He turned Prince into the track behind the swaying sleigh. The black horse seemed immediately to scent the chase. He snorted and increased his stride.

"Oh, Walter! Can you catch them?" Nan cried.

"I bet Prince can," the boy replied, between his set teeth.

The policeman on horseback was of course ahead in the chase after the runaways. But the snow on this side road was softer than on the speedway, and it balled under his horse's hoofs.

The black horse driven by Walter Mason was more sure-footed than the policeman's mount. The latter slipped and lost its stride. Prince went past the floundering horse like a flash.

The swaying sleigh was just ahead now. Walter drew Prince to one side so that the cutter would clear the sleigh in passing.

The chums could see poor, frightened Linda crouching in the bottom of the sleigh, clinging with both hands to one of the straps from which the plumes streamed. Her face was white and she looked almost ready to faint.

CHAPTER XXVI

AN UNEXPECTED FIND

The mounted policeman came thundering down the street after them, his horse having regained its footing. The reins of the big steeds were dragging on the ground, and Walter and his girl companions saw no way of getting hold of the lines and so pulling down the frightened horses.

There was another way to save Linda Riggs, however. Walter looked at Nan

Sherwood and his lips moved.

"Are you afraid to drive Prince?" he asked.

"No," declared Nan, and reached for the reins. She had held the black horse before. Besides, she had driven her Cousin Tom's pair of big draught horses up in the Michigan woods, and Mr. Henry Sherwood's half-wild roan ponies, as well. Her wrists were strong and supple, and she was alert.

Walter passed the lines over and then kicked the robe out of the way. Bess sat on the left side of the seat, clinging to the rail. She was frightened—but more for the girl in the other sleigh, than because of their own danger.

Walter Mason motioned to Bess to move over to Nan's side. The latter was guiding Prince carefully, and the cutter crept up beside the bigger vehicle. Only a couple of feet separated the two sleighs as Walter leaned out from his own seat and shouted to Linda:

"Look this way! Look! Do exactly as I tell you!"

The girl turned her strained face toward him. The bigger sleigh swerved and almost collided with the cutter.

"Now!" yelled Walter, excitedly. "Let go!"

He had seized Linda by the arm, clinging with his other hand to the rail of the cutter-seat. She screamed—and so did Bess.

But Walter's grasp was strong, and, after all, Linda was not heavy. Her hold was torn from the plume-staff, and she was half lifted, half dragged, into the cutter.

Prince darted past the now laboring runaways. One of the latter slipped on a smooth bit of ice and crashed to the roadway.

His mate went down with him and the sleigh was overturned. Had Linda not been rescued as she was, her injury—perhaps her death—would have been certain.

They stopped at the first drug store and a man held the head of the excited black horse while Walter soothed and blanketed him. Then the boy went inside, and into the prescription room, where Nan and Bess were comforting their schoolmate.

"Oh, dear! oh, dear! I'd have been killed if it hadn't been for you, Walter Mason," cried Linda, for once so thoroughly shaken out of her pose that she acted and spoke naturally. "How can I ever thank you enough?"

"Say!" blurted out Walter. "You'd better thank Nan, here, too. I couldn't have grabbed you if it hadn't been for her. She held Prince and guided the sleigh."

"Oh, that's all right!" interjected Nan, at once very much embarrassed. "Anybody would have done the same."

"'Tisn't so!" cried Bess. "I just held on and squealed."

But Linda's pride was quite broken down. She looked at Nan with her own eyes streaming.

"Oh, Sherwood!" she murmured. "I've said awfully mean things about you. I'm so sorry—I really am."

"Oh, that's all right!" muttered Nan, almost boyish in her confusion.

"Well, I have! I know I made fun of your medal for bravery. You deserve another for what you just did. Oh, dear! I—I never can thank any of you enough;" and she cried again on Bess Harley's shoulder.

Walter telephoned to the Graves' house, telling Linda's aunt of the accident and of Linda's predicament, and when a vehicle was sent for the hysterical girl the boy, with Nan and Bess, hurried home to a late luncheon, behind black Prince.

Although Mrs. Mason, naturally, was disturbed over the risk of accident Walter and the girl chums had taken in rescuing Linda Riggs, the interest of the young folks was in, and all their comment upon, the possible change of heart the purse-proud girl had undergone.

"I don't know about these 'last hour conversions,'" said the pessimistic Bess. "I should wring the tears out of the shoulder of my coat and bottle 'em. Only tears I ever heard of Linda's shedding! And they may prove to be crocodile tears at that."

"Oh, hush, Bess!" said Nan. "Let's not be cruel."

"We'll see how she treats you hereafter," Grace said. "I, for one, hope Linda *has* had a change of heart. She'll be so much happier if she stops quarreling with everybody."

"And the other girls will have a little more peace, too, I fancy; eh?" threw in her brother, slyly. "But how about this place you want to go to this afternoon, Nan?" he added.

"I should think you had had enough excitement for one day," Mrs. Mason sighed. "The wonderful vitality of these young creatures! It amazes me. They wish to be on the go all of the time."

"You see," Nan explained, "we have only a few more days in Chicago and I am *so* desirous of finding Sallie and Celia. Poor Mrs. Morton is heart-broken, and I expect Celia's mother fears all the time for her daughter's safety, too."

"Those foolish girls!" Mrs. Mason said. "I am glad you young people haven't this general craze for exhibiting one's self in moving pictures."

"You can't tell when that may begin, Mother," chuckled Walter. "When Nan was holding on to Prince and I was dragging Linda out of that sleigh, if a camera-man had been along he could have made some picture—believe me!"

"You'll walk or take a car to the address," Mrs. Mason instructed them. "No more riding behind that excited horse to-day, please."

Nan Sherwood's Winter Holidays

"All right, Mother," said Walter, obediently. "Now, whenever you girls are ready, I am at your service. It's lucky I know pretty well the poorer localities in Chicago. Your calling district, Nan Sherwood, seems to number in it a lot of shady localities."

However, it was only a poor neighborhood, not a vicious one, in which Jennie Albert lived. Grace had accompanied the chums from Tillbury, and the trio of girls went along very merrily with Walter until they came near to the number Mr. Gray had given them.

This number they had some difficulty in finding. At least, four hundred and sixteen was a big warehouse in which nobody lodged of course. Plenty of tenement houses crowded about it but four hundred and sixteen was surely the warehouse.

While Walter was inquiring in some of the little neighboring stores, Nan saw a child pop out of a narrow alley beside the warehouse and look sharply up and down the street. It was the furtive, timid glance of the woods creature or the urchin of the streets; both expect and fear the attack of the strong.

The Lakeview Hall girls were across the street. The little girl darted suddenly toward them. Her head was covered by an old shawl, which half blinded her. Her garments were scanty for such brisk winter weather, and her shoes were broken.

"Oh, the poor little thing!" murmured Grace Mason.

Nan was suddenly excited by the sight of the child crossing the crowded street; she sprang to the edge of the walk, but did not scream as the little one scurried on. Down the driveway came a heavy auto-truck and although the little girl saw the approach of this, she could not well see what followed the great vehicle.

She escaped the peril of the truck, but came immediately in the path of a touring car that shot out from behind to pass the truck. With a nerve-racking "honk! honk!" the swiftly moving car was upon the child.

Bess and Grace *did* scream; but Nan, first aware of the little one's danger, was likewise first to attempt her rescue. And she needed her breath for that effort. Other people shouted at the child and, from either sidewalk, Nan was the only person who darted out to save her!

The driver under the steering wheel of the touring car did his best to bring it to an abrupt stop; but the wheels skidded and—for a breathless moment—it did seem as though the shawl-blinded child must go under the wheels of the vehicle.

Nan Sherwood seized the shawl and by main strength dragged its owner to the gutter. The car slid past; both girls were safe!

"You lemme be! you lemme be!" shrieked the girl Nan had rescued, evidently considering herself much abused by the rough treatment her rescuer had given her, and struggling all the time to keep Nan from lifting her upon the sidewalk.

"Why, you little savage!" gasped Bess Harley. "Don't you know you've been saved?"

"Who wants to be saved?" demanded the smaller girl, looking up at the three older ones out of the hood of the shawl she had clung to so desperately. "What youse savin' me *from*?"

Bess grew more excited. "Why, Nan!" she cried. "It is—it must be! Don't you see who she is?"

Nan was already looking down into the dark, shrewd and thin countenance of the little one with a smile of recognition. It was Inez, the little flower-girl, whom she had so fortunately pulled out of the way of the automobile.

"Hullo, honey; don't you know us?" Nan asked her.

"Hi!" exclaimed the street waif. "If it ain't me tony friends from Washington Park. Say! youse got ter excuse me. I didn't know youse."

"Why, Inez!" exclaimed Nan, kindly. "You have a dreadful cold."

"Say! if I don't have nothin' worse than that I'll do fine," croaked the little girl, carelessly. "But I never expected to see youse tony folks again."

"Why, Inez!" exclaimed Bess. "And we've been hunting all over for you."

"Goodness me!" burst out Grace Mason. "You don't mean to say that this is the poor little thing we've been in such a fuss about?"

"Of course she is," Bess replied.

"This is positively Inez," laughed Nan, squeezing the little one's cold hand in her own. "Aren't you glad to see us, child?"

"I dunno," said Inez, doubtfully. "Youse ain't come to take me back to me aunt, have youse?" and she looked around for a chance to escape. "I ain't goin' to live with her no more—now I tell youse!" and she became quite excited.

Nan sought to reassure her. "Don't you be afraid, honey. We wouldn't see you abused. We only want to help you. That is why we have been searching for you."

"You been huntin' me up—jest to *help* me?" gasped Inez, in wonder.

"Of course we have," said Bess.

"Hi!" exclaimed the flower-seller, with an impish grin. "I reckon me aunt would say some of yer buttons was missin'. Youse can't be right in the upper story," and she pointed to her own head to illustrate her meaning.

"Goodness!" gasped Grace. "Does she think we are crazy because we want to do her a kindness?"

"She's not used to being treated with much consideration, I am afraid," Nan observed, in a low voice.

"You ridiculous child!" came from Bess. "Don't you know that we were both interested in you that first day? We told you we would see you again."

"Aw, that don't mean nothin'," sniffed Inez. "I didn't expect nothin' would come of it. If youse folks from Washington Park ain't crazy, what is the matter wit' youse? I ain't nothin' ter you."

"Why, goodness me!" cried Grace again. "Do you think everybody who is kind must be out of his head? Who ever heard the like?"

"Folks ain't generally crazy to do me no favors," said Inez, with one of her sharp glances. "But if you girls want ter give me somethin' for nothin,' you've lost some of yer buttons, that's sure!"

Nan and her two companions had to laugh at this, but the laughter was close to tears, after all. It was really pathetic that this waif of the streets should suspect the sanity of anybody who desired to do her a kindness.

CHAPTER XXVII

JENNIE ALBERT—AND SOMEBODY ELSE

"Well! what do you know about that?" was Walter's comment, when he came back to the girls and found them surrounding the hungry looking little street waif, of whom he had already heard so much from Nan and Bess.

"We go out to shoot partridges and bring down a crow," he added. "Goodness! what a hungry looking kid. There's a bakeshop over the way. Bring her in and see if we can't cure this child of old Father Famine."

Inez looked at Walter askance at first. But when she understood that he was going to stand treat to coffee and cakes, she grew friendlier.

"Yep, I'm hungry," she admitted. "Ain't I *always* hungry? M-m—!" as the shop door opened and she sniffed the odors of coffee and food.

"Do, *do* hurry and feed the poor little thing," urged Grace, almost in tears. "Oh! I'm sorry I came with you girls. Hungry! Only think of being *hungry*, Walter!"

Inez looked at Grace as though she thought she was losing her mind.

"Aw, say," said she, "don't let it worry youse. I'm uster being empty, *I* am. And 'specially since me and me aunt had our fallin' out."

"Oh! we know about that, Inez," cried Bess. "We went there to look for you."

"To me aunt's?" asked Inez, in some excitement.

"Yes," Nan replied.

"Is she a-lookin' for me?" demanded the child with a restless glance at the door of the shop.

"I don't think she is," Nan said.

"I should say not!" Bess added. "She seems to fairly hate you, child. And didn't she beat you?"

"Yep. She's the biggest, ye see. She took away all me money and then burned me basket. That was puttin' me on the fritz for fair, and I went wild and went for her. This is what I got!"

She dropped the shawl off her head suddenly. There, above the temple and where the tangled black hair had been cut away, was a long, angry wound. It was partially healed.

"Oh, my dear!" cried Nan.

Grace fell to crying. Bess grew very angry and threatened all manner of punishments for the cruel aunt.

"How did she do it?" Walter asked.

"Flat iron," replied the waif, succinctly. "I had the poker. She 'got' me first. I didn't dare go back, and I thought I'd die that first night."

"Oh, oh!" sobbed Grace. "Out in the cold, too!"

"Yes'm," Inez said, eating and drinking eagerly. "But a nice feller in a drug store—a night clerk, I guess youse call him—took me in after one o'clock, an' give me something to eat, and fixed up me head."

"What a kind man!" exclaimed Bess.

"So you see, Inez, there are some kind folks in the world," said Nan, smiling at the waif. "Some kind ones beside *us*."

"Yep," the child admitted. "But not rich folks like youse."

"Goodness, child!" gasped Grace. "We're not rich."

Inez stared at her with a mouthful poised upon her knife. "Cracky!" she ejaculated. "What do youse call it? Furs, and fine dresses, and nothin' ter do but sport around—Hi! if youse girls from Washington Park ain't rich, what d'ye call it?"

Nan was looking serious again. "I guess the child is right," she said, with a little sigh. "We *are* rich. Compared with what *she* has, we're as rich as old King Midas."

"For goodness' sake!" cried Bess. "I hope *not*—at least, not in ears."

The others laughed; but Nan added: "I guess we don't realize how well off we are."

"Hear! hear!" murmured Walter. "Being sure of three meals a day would be riches to this poor little thing."

"Hi!" ejaculated Inez, still eating greedily. "That'd be *Heaven*, that would!"

"But do let her finish her story, girls," urged Bess. "Go on, dear. What happened to you after the kind druggist took you in?"

"I staid all night there," said Inez. "He fixed me a bunk on an old lounge in the back room. An' next morning a girl I useter see at Mother Beasley's seen me and brought me over here. She ain't well now and her money's about run out, I reckon. Say! did youse ever find them two greenies youse was lookin' for?" she suddenly asked Nan.

"Oh, no! We're looking for them now," Nan replied. "Have you seen them, Inez?"

"I dunno. I b'lieve my friend may know something about them."

"You mean the girl you are with?" Nan asked.

"Yep."

"Who is she?" asked Bess.

"She's one o' them movin' picture actorines. She does stunts."

"'Stunts'?" repeated Walter, while Nan and Bess looked at each other with interest. "What sort of 'stunts,' pray?"

"Hard jobs. Risky ones, too. And that last one she went out on she got an awful cold. Whew! I been expectin' her to cough herself to pieces."

"But what did she do?" repeated the curious Walter.

"Oh, she was out in the country with the X.L.Y. Company. She was playin' a boy's part—she's as thin as I am, but tall and lanky. Makes up fine as a boy," said Inez, with some enthusiasm.

"She was supposed to be a boy helpin' some robbers. They put her through a ventilator into a sleepin' car standin' in the railroad yards. That's where she got cold," Inez added, "for she had to dress awful light so's to wiggle through the ventilator winder. It was a cold mornin', an' she came back ter town 'most dead."

"Where is she now?" asked Walter.

But it was Nan's question which brought out the most surprising response. "Who is she?" Nan asked the little girl. "What is her name?"

"Jennie Albert. An' she's a sure 'nough movie girl, too. But she can't get good jobs because she ain't pretty."

"I declare!" exclaimed Bess, finally, after a moment of surprised silence.

"I know she can't live over there in that big warehouse, and that's number four hundred and sixteen," said Grace.

"She lives in a house back in a court beside that big one," explained Inez. "It's four hundred and sixteen *and a half*."

"Then it's only half a house?" suggested Bess Harley.

"I know it can be only *half* fit to live in," said Walter. "Not many of these around here are. What are you going to do now, Nan?"

"Inez will take us over and introduce us to Jennie."

"Sure thing!" agreed the waif.

"Tell us, Inez," Nan said. "What can we take in to your friend Jennie?"

"To eat, or comforts of any kind?" cried Grace, opening her purse at once.

"Hi!" cried Inez. "Jest look around. Anything youse see. *She ain't got nothin'*."

"Which was awful grammar, but the most illuminating sentence I ever heard," declared Bess, afterward.

The girls made special inquiries of the child, however, and they did more than carry over something for the sick girl to eat. They bought an oil heater and a big can of oil, for the girl's room was unheated.

There was extra bed-clothing and some linen to get, too, for Inez was an observant little thing and knew just what the sick girl needed.

Walter meanwhile bought fresh fruit and canned goods—soup and preserved fruit—and a jar of calf's foot jelly.

The procession that finally took up its march into the alley toward number four hundred and sixteen *and a half*, headed by Inez and with the boy from the shop bearing the heater and the oil can as rear guard, was an imposing one indeed.

"See what I brought you, Jen Albert!" cried Inez, as she burst in the door of the poorly furnished room. "These are some of me tony friends from Washington Park, and they've come to have a picnic."

The room was as cheaply and meanly furnished as any that the three girls from Lakeview Hall had ever seen. Nan thought she had seen poverty of household goods and furnishings when she had lived for a season with her Uncle Henry Sherwood at Pine Camp, in the woods of Upper Michigan. Some of the neighbors there had scarcely a factory made chair to sit on. But this room in which Jennie Albert lived, and to which she had brought the little flower-seller for shelter, was so barren and ugly that it made Nan shudder as she gazed at it.

The girl who rose suddenly off the ragged couch as the three friends entered, startled them even more than the appearance of the room itself. She was so thin and haggard—she had such red, red cheeks—such feverish eyes—such an altogether wild and distraught air—that timid Grace shrank back and looked at Walter, who remained with the packages and bundles at the head of the stairs.

Nan and Bess likewise looked at the girl with some trepidation; but they held their ground.

"What do you want? Who are you?" asked Jennie Albert, hoarsely.

"We—we have come to see you," explained Nan, hesitatingly. "We're friends of little Inez."

"You'd better keep away from here!" cried the older girl, fiercely. "This is no place for the likes of you."

"Aw, say! Now, don't get flighty again, Jen," urged little Inez, much worried. "I tell youse these girls is all right. Why, they're pertic'lar friends of mine."

"Your—your friends?" muttered the wild looking girl. "This—this is a poor place to bring your friends, Ina. But—do sit down! Do take a chair!"

She waved her hand toward the only chair there was—a broken-armed parlor chair, the upholstery of which was in rags. She laughed as she did so—a sudden, high, cackling laugh. Then she broke out coughing and—as Inez had said—she seemed in peril of shaking herself to pieces!

"Oh, the poor thing!" murmured Bess to Nan.

"She is dreadfully ill," the latter whispered. "She ought really to have a doctor right now."

"Oh, girls!" gasped Grace, in terror. "Let's come away. Perhaps she has some contagious disease. She looks just *awful*!"

The sick girl heard this, low as the three visitors spoke. "And I feel 'just awful!'" she gasped, when she got her breath after coughing. "You'd better not stay to visit Ina. This is no place for you."

"Why, we must do something to help you," Nan declared, recovering some of her assurance. "Surely you should have a doctor."

"He gimme some medicine for her yesterday," broke in Inez. "But we ain't got no more money for medicine. Has we, Jen?"

"Not much for anything else, either," muttered the bigger girl, turning her face away.

She was evidently ashamed of her poverty. Nan saw that it irked Jennie Albert to have strangers see her need and she hastened, as usual, to relieve the girl of that embarrassment.

"My dear," she said, running to her as Jennie sat on the couch, and putting an arm about the poor, thin, shaking shoulders. "My dear! we would not disturb you only that you may be able to help us find two lost girls. And you *are* so sick. Do let us stay a while and help you, now that we have come, in return for the information you can give us about Sallie Morton and Celia Snubbins."

"Gracious! who are they?" returned Jennie Albert. "I never heard of them, I'm sure," and she seemed to speak quite naturally for a moment.

"Oh, my dear!" murmured Nan. "Haven't you seen them at all? Why, they told me at the studio—"

"I know! I know!" exclaimed Bess, suddenly. "Jennie doesn't know their right names. Nan means Lola Montague and Marie Fortesque."

Jennie Albert stared wonderingly at them. "Why—*those* girls? I remember them, of course," she said. "I supposed those names were assumed, but I had no idea they really owned such ugly ones."

"And where, for goodness' sake, are they?" cried the impatient Bess.

"Miss Montague and her friend?"

"Yes," Nan explained. "We are very anxious to find them, and have been looking for them ever since we came to Chicago. You see, they have run away from home, Jennie, and their parents are terribly worried about them."

"Maybe they were ill-treated at home," Jennie Albert said, gloomily.

"Oh, they were not!" cried Bess, eagerly. "We know better. Poor old Si Snubbins thinks just the world and all of Celia."

"And Mrs. Morton is one of the loveliest women I ever met," Nan added. "The girls have just gone crazy over the movies."

"Over acting in them, do you mean?" asked the girl who "did stunts."

"Yes. And they can't act. Mr. Gray says so."

"Oh, if they were no good he'd send them packing in a hurry," groaned the sick girl, holding her head with both hands. "I sent them over to him because I knew he wanted at least *one* extra."

"And he did not even take their address," Nan explained. "Do you know where they live?"

"No, I don't. They just happened in here. I know that they recently moved from a former lodging they had on the other side of town. That is really all I know about them," said Jennie Albert.

Meanwhile Walter had been quietly handing in the packages to his sister and Bess. The oil stove was deftly filled by the good-hearted boy before he lifted it and the can of oil inside.

When the big lamp was lit the chill of the room was soon dispelled. Little Inez opened the packages eagerly, chattering all the time to Jennie Albert about the good things the young folks from Washington Park had brought.

But the sick girl, after her little show of interest in Nan's questioning, quickly fell back into a lethargic state. Nan whispered to Inez and asked her about the doctor she had seen for Jennie.

"Is he a good one?" she asked the child. "And will he come here if we pay him?"

"He's a corker!" exclaimed the street waif. "But he's mighty busy. You got to show him money in your hand to get him to come to see anybody. You know how these folks are around here. They don't have no money for nothin'—least of all for doctors."

She told Nan where the busy physician was to be found, and Nan whispered to Walter the address and sent him hurrying for the man of pills and powders.

Until the doctor returned with Walter the girls busied themselves cleaning up the room, undressing the patient, and putting her into bed between fresh sheets, and making her otherwise more comfortable. There was a good woman on this same floor of the old tenement house, and Grace paid her out of her own purse to look in on Jennie Albert occasionally and see that she got her medicine and food.

For they were all determined not to leave little Inez in these poor lodgings. "Goodness knows," Bess remarked, "if she gets out of our sight now we may never find her again. She's just as elusive as a flea!"

The child looked at Bess in her sly, wondering way, and said: "Hi! I never had nobody worry over what become of me 'fore this. Seems like it's somethin' new."

CHAPTER XXVIII

WHAT HAPPENED TO INEZ

Walter, who had gone downstairs to wait after he had brought the doctor, had a long wait in the cold court at the door of the lodging house in which Jennie Albert lived. A less patient and good-natured boy would have been angry when his sister and her school chums finally appeared.

He was glad that Grace took an interest in anything besides her own pleasure and comfort. His sister, Walter thought, was too much inclined to dodge responsibility and everything unpleasant.

He wanted her to be more like Nan. "But, then," the boy thought, "there's only one Nan Sherwood in the world. Guess I can't expect Grace to run a very close second to her."

However, when the girls did appear Grace was chattering just as excitedly as Bess Harley herself; and she led Inez by the hand.

"Yes, she shall! She'll go right home with me now—sha'n't she, Walter?" Grace cried. "You get a taxi, and we'll all pile in—did you ever ride in a taxi, Inez?"

"Nope. But I caught on behind a jitney once," confessed the little girl, "and a cop bawled me out for it."

"We're going to take her home, and dress her up nice," Bess explained to Walter, "and give her the time of her life."

Inez seemed a bit dazed. In her own vernacular she would probably have said—had she found her voice—that "things was comin' too fast for her." She scarcely knew what these girls intended to do with her; but she had a good deal of confidence in Nan Sherwood, and she looked back at her frequently.

It was to Nan, too, that Walter looked for directions as to their further movements, as well as for exact information as to what had gone on up stairs in Jennie Albert's room.

"She's an awfully plucky girl," Nan said. "No; she's not very ill now," the doctor said, "but she does have a dreadful cough. However, the doctor has given her medicine.

"It's odd," Nan added thoughtfully, "but she got this cold down at Tillbury. The company she was out with were taking pictures near there. There's a big old mansion called the Coscommon House that hasn't been occupied for years. It's often filmed by movie people; but never in the winter before, that I know of."

"But, Nan!" exclaimed Walter. "What did we come over here for, anyway? How about those runaway girls?"

"I'm sorry," Nan said, shaking her head; "but we haven't found them. They don't live here, and Jennie doesn't know where they do live."

"Goodness! What elusive creatures they are," grumbled Walter.

"Aren't they!" Bess exclaimed. "Jennie Albert just happened to meet them when they were looking for work, and told them where she lived. So they came around to see her the other day. That Mr. Gray we saw at the studio had just sent for Jennie, and so she told them to go around and see him. Yes! Just think! 'Lola Montague' and 'Marie Fortesque'! Say! Aren't those names the limit?"

But Nan considered the matter too serious to joke about. "I am afraid that Sallie and Celia must be about to *their* limit," she said. "Poor Mrs. Morton! She said Sallie was stubborn, and she must be, to endure so many disappointments and not give up and go home."

"The sillies!" said Walter. "How about it, kid? Would *you* run away from a good home, even if it were in the country?"

"Not if the eats came reg'lar and they didn't beat me too much," declared Inez, repeating her former declaration.

"Well, then, we'll take you where the 'eats' at least come regular," laughed Walter. "Eh, Grace?"

"Of course. Do hurry and get that taxi."

"What do you suppose your mother will say, Grace?" demanded Bess, in sudden doubt, when Walter had departed to telephone for the taxi-cab.

"I know mother will pity the poor little soul," Grace declared. "I'm sure she belongs to enough charitable boards and committees so that she ought to be delighted that we bring a real 'case,' as she calls them, to her," and Grace laughed at her own conceit.

Nan, however, wondered if, after all, Mrs. Mason would care to take any practical responsibility upon herself regarding the street waif. It was one thing to be theoretically charitable and an entirely different matter to take a case of deserving charity into one's own home.

But that thought did not disturb Nan. She had already planned a future for little Inez. She was determined to take her back to Tillbury and leave Inez with her mother.

"I'm sure," Nan said to herself, "that Momsey will be glad to have a little girl around the house again. And Inez can go to school, and grow to be good and polite. For, goodness knows! she *is* a little savage now."

Eventually these dreams of Nan for little Inez came true. Just at present, however, much more material things happened to her when they arrived at the Mason house.

Grace and Bess hung over the little girl, and fussed about her, as Walter laughingly said, "like a couple of hens over one chicken."

Nan was glad to see her schoolmates so much interested in the waif. She knew it would do both Grace and Bess good to have their charitable emotions awakened.

As for Mrs. Mason, Nan soon saw that that kindly lady would be both helpful and wise in the affair. Left to their own desires, Grace and Bess would have dressed Inez up like a French doll. But Nan told Mrs. Mason privately just what she hoped to do with the child, and the lady heartily approved.

"A very good thing—very good, indeed, Nan Sherwood," said Mrs. Mason, "if your father and mother approve."

As it chanced, there was a letter from Mrs. Sherwood awaiting Nan when she and her schoolmates arrived with Inez; from it Nan learned that her father would be in Chicago the next day, having been called to a final conference with the heads of the automobile corporation.

"Mr. Bulson is so insistent, and is so ugly," the letter said, "that I fear your dear father will have to go to court. It will be a great expense as well as a notorious affair.

"Fighting an accusation that you cannot disprove is like Don Quixote's old fight with the windmill. There is nothing to be gained in the end. It is a dreadful, dreadful thing."

Nan determined to meet her father and tell him all about Inez. She was sure he would be interested in the waif, and in her plans for Inez's future.

That night, however, at the Mason house, there was much excitement among the young people. Of course the girls got Katie, the maid, to help with Inez. Katie would have done anything for Nan, if not for Grace herself; and although she did not at first quite approve of the street waif, she ended in loving Inez.

In the first place they bathed the child and wrapped her in a soft, fleecy gown of Grace's. Her clothing, every stitch of it, was carried gingerly down to the basement by Katie, and burned.

From the garments Mrs. Harley had sent a complete outfit for the child was selected. They were probably the best garments Inez had ever worn.

"She looks as nice now as me own sister," Katie declared, when, after a deal of fussing and chatting in the girls' suite, the street waif was dressed from top to toe.

"Now ye may take her down to show the mistress; and I belave she will be plazed."

This was a true prophecy. Not only was Mrs. Mason delighted with the changed appearance of Inez, but Mr. Mason approved, too; while Walter considered the metamorphosis quite marvelous.

"Great!" he said. "Get her filled up, and filled out, and her appearance alone will pay you girls for your trouble."

While they talked and joked about her, Inez fell fast asleep with her head pillowed in Nan Sherwood's lap.

CHAPTER XXIX

THE KEY TO A HARD LOCK

The young people had planned to spend that next forenoon at a skating rink, where the ice was known to be good; but Nan ran away right after breakfast to meet her father's train, intending to join the crowd at the rink later.

"I'll take your skates for you, Nan," Walter assured her, as she set forth for the station.

"That's so kind of you, Walter," she replied gratefully.

"Say! I'd do a whole lot more for you than *that*," blurted out the boy, his face reddening.

"I think you have already," said Nan, sweetly, waving him good-bye from the taxi in which Mrs. Mason had insisted she should go to the station.

She settled back in her seat and thought happily for a few minutes. She had been so busy with all sorts of things here in Chicago—especially with what Bess Harley called "other people's worries"—that Nan had scarcely been able to think of her hopes for the future, or her memories of the past. She had been living very much in the present.

"Why," she thought, with something like a feeling of remorse, "I haven't even missed Beautiful Beulah. I—I wonder if I am really growing up? Oh, dear!"

Mr. Sherwood thought her a very much composed and sophisticated little body, indeed, when he met her on the great concourse of the railway station.

"Goodness me, Nan!" he declared, when he had greeted her. "How you *do* grow. Your mother and I have seen so little of you since we came back from Scotland, that we haven't begun to realize that you are a big, big girl."

"Don't make me out *too* big, Papa Sherwood!" she cried, clinging to his arm. "I—I don't *want* to grow up entirely. I want for a long time to be *your* little girl.

"I know what we'll do," cried Nan, delightedly. "You have plenty of time before your business conference. We'll walk along together to see how Jennie Albert is—it isn't far from here—and you shall buy me a bag of peanuts, just as you used to do, and we'll eat 'em right on the street as we go along."

"Is that the height of your ambition?" laughed Mr. Sherwood. "If so, you are easily satisfied."

Nan told her father all about the search for the runaway girls, and about little Inez and Jennie Albert. She wanted to see how the latter was. The comforts she and her friends had left the sick girl the day before, and the ministrations of the physician, should have greatly improved Jennie's condition.

Nan left her father at the entrance to the alley leading back to Jennie's lodging; but in a few minutes she came flying back to Mr. Sherwood in such excitement that at first she could scarcely speak connectedly.

"Why, Nan! What is the matter?" her father demanded.

"Oh! come up and see Jennie! *Do* come up and see Jennie!" urged Nan.

"What is the matter with her? Is she worse?"

"Oh, no! Oh, no!" cried the excited girl. "But she has got such a wonderful thing to tell you, Papa Sherwood!"

"To tell me?" asked her father wonderingly.

"Yes! Come!" Nan seized his hand and pulled him into the alley. On the way she explained a little of the mystery.

"Dear me! it's the most wonderful thing, Papa Sherwood. You know, I told you Jennie was working for a moving picture company that was making a film at Tillbury. She had a boy's part; she looks just like a boy with a cap on, for her hair is short.

"Well! Now listen! They took those pictures the day before, and the very day that you came back from Chicago to Tillbury and that awful Mr. Bulson lost his money and watch."

"What's that?" demanded Mr. Sherwood, suddenly evincing all the interest Nan expected him to in the tale.

As they mounted the stairs Nan retailed how the company had gone to the railroad yards early in the morning, obtaining permission from the yardmaster to film a scene outside the sleeping car standing there on a siding, including the entrance of Jennie as the burglars' helper through the narrow ventilator.

"Of course, the sleeping car doors can only be opened from the inside when it is occupied, save with a key," Nan hastened to say; "so you see she was supposed to enter through the ventilator and afterward open the door to the men."

"I see," Mr. Sherwood observed, yet still rather puzzled by his daughter's vehemence.

Jennie Albert, however, when he was introduced to her by Nan, gave a much clearer account of the matter. To take up the story where Nan had broken off, Jennie, when she wriggled through the window into the car, had seen a big negro man stooping over a man in a lower berth and removing something from under his pillow.

The man in the berth was lying on his back and snoring vociferously. There seemed to be no other passenger remaining in the car.

Jennie did not see what the colored man took from the sleeping passenger, but she was sure he was robbing him. The negro, however, saw Jennie, and threatened to harm her if she ever spoke of the matter.

The director of the picture and other men were outside. The girl was alarmed and more than half sick then. She had the remainder of the director's instructions to carry out.

Therefore, she hurried to open the sleeping car door as her instructions called for, and the negro thief escaped without Jennie's saying a word to anybody about him.

Mr. Sherwood, as deeply interested, but calmer than Nan, asked questions to make sure of the identity of the sleeping passenger. It was Mr. Ravell Bulson, without a doubt.

"And about the negro?" he asked the girl. "Describe him."

But all Jennie could say was that he was a big, burly fellow with a long, long nose.

"An awfully long nose for a colored person," said Jennie. "He frightened me so, I don't remember much else about him—and I'm no scare-cat, either. You ask any of the directors I have worked for during the past two years. If I only had a pretty face like your Nan, here, Mr. Sherwood, they'd be giving me the lead in feature films—believe me!"

The mystery of how the negro got into the locked car was explained when Mr. Sherwood chanced to remember that the porter of the coach in which he had ridden from Chicago that night answered the description Jennie Albert gave of the person who had robbed Mr. Bulson.

"I remember that nose!" declared Mr. Sherwood, with satisfaction. "Now we'll clear this mystery up. You have given me a key, Miss Jennie, to what was a very hard lock to open."

This proved to be true. Mr. Sherwood went to his conference with the automobile people with a lighter heart. On their advice, he told the story to the police and the description of the negro porter was recognized as that of a man who already had a police record—one "Nosey" Thompson.

This negro had obtained a position with the sleeping car company under a false name and with fraudulent recommendations.

These facts Nan, at least, did not learn till later; she ran off to the skating rink, secure in the thought that her father's trouble with Mr. Ravell Bulson was over. She hoped she might never see that grouchy fat man again. But Fate had in store for her another meeting with the disagreeable Mr. Bulson, and this fell out in a most surprising way.

When Nan was almost in sight of the building where she expected to join her friends on skates, there sounded the sudden clangor of firetruck whistles, and all other traffic halted to allow the department machines to pass. A taxi-cab crowded close in to the curb where Nan had halted, just as the huge ladder-truck, driven by its powerful motor, swung around the corner.

Pedestrians, of course, had scattered to the sidewalks; but the wheels of the ladder-truck skidded on the icy street and the taxi was caught a glancing blow by the rear wheel of the heavier vehicle.

Many of the onlookers screamed warnings in chorus; but all to no avail. Indeed, there was nothing the driver of the cab could have done to avert the catastrophe. His engine was stopped and there was no possibility of escape with the car.

Crash! the truck-wheel clashed against the frail cab, and the latter vehicle was crushed as though made of paper. The driver went out on his head. Screams of fear issued from the interior of the cab as it went over in a heap of wreckage and the ladder-truck thundered on.

Nan saw a fat face with bulging eyes set in it appear at the window of the cab. She was obliged to spring away to escape being caught in the wreck. But she ran back instantly, for there were more than the owner of the fat face in the overturned taxi.

With the sputtering of the fat man there sounded, too, a shrill, childish scream of fear, and a wild yelp of pain—the latter unmistakably from a canine throat. Amid the wreckage Nan beheld a pair of blue-stockinged legs encased in iron supports; but the dog wriggled free.

"Hey! Hey!" roared the fat man. "Help us out of this. Never mind that driver. He ought to have seen that thing coming and got out of the way. Hey! Help us out, I say."

Nobody seemed to be paying much attention to the fat and angry citizen; nor would Nan have heeded him had it not been for the appeal of those two blue-stockinged legs in the iron braces.

The fat man was all tangled up in the robes and in the broken fittings of the cab. He could do nothing for himself, let alone assist in the rescue of the owner of the crippled little limbs. The dog, darting about, barked wildly.

As Nan stooped to lift the broken cab door off the apparently injured boy, the dog—he was only a puppy—ran yapping at her in a fever of apprehension. But his barking suddenly changed to yelps of joy as he leaped on Nan and licked her hands.

"Why, Buster!" gasped the girl, recognizing the little spaniel that she and Bess Harley had befriended in the snow-bound train.

She knew instantly, then, whose was the fat and apoplectic face; but she did not understand about the legs in the cruel looking iron braces until she had drawn a small and sharp-featured lad of seven or eight years of age from under the debris of the taxi-cab.

"Jingo! Look at Pop!" exclaimed the crippled boy, who seemed not to have been hurt at all in the accident.

Mr. Ravell Bulson was trying to struggle out from under the cab. And to his credit he was not thinking of himself at this time.

"How's Junior?" he gasped. "Are you hurt, Junior?"

"No, Pop, I ain't hurt," said the boy with the braces. "But, Jingo! you do look funny."

"I don't feel so funny," snarled his parent, finally extricating himself unaided from the tangle. "Sure you're not hurt, Junior?"

"No, I'm not hurt," repeated the boy. "Nor Buster ain't hurt. And see this girl, Pop. Buster knows her."

Mr. Ravell Bulson just then obtained a clear view of Nan Sherwood, against whom the little dog was crazily leaping. The man scowled and in his usual harsh manner exclaimed:

"Call the dog away, Junior. If you're not hurt we'll get another cab and go on."

"Why, Pop!" cried the lame boy, quite excitedly. "That pup likes her a whole lot. See him? Say, girl, did you used to own that puppy?"

"No, indeed, dear," said Nan, laughing. "But he remembers me."

"From where?" demanded the curious Ravell Bulson, Jr.

"Why, since the time we were snow-bound in a train together."

"Oh! when was that?" burst out the boy. "Tell me about it snowbound in a steam-car train? That must have been jolly."

"Come away, Junior!" exclaimed his father. "You don't care anything about that, I'm sure."

"Oh, yes I do, Pop. I want to hear about it. Fancy being snow-bound in a steam-car train!"

"Come away, I tell you," said the fat man, again scowling crossly at Nan. "You don't want to hear anything that girl can tell you. Come away, now," he added, for a crowd was gathering.

"Do wait a minute, Pop," said Junior. The lame boy evidently was used to being indulged, and he saw no reason for leaving Nan abruptly. "See the dog. See Buster, will you? Why, he's just in love with this girl."

"I tell you to come on!" complained Mr. Bulson, Senior. He was really a slave to the crippled boy's whims; but he disliked being near Nan Sherwood, or seeing Junior so friendly with her. "You can't know that girl, if the dog does," he snarled.

"Why, yes I can, Pop," said the lame boy, with cheerful insistence. "And I want to hear about her being snowed up in a train with Buster."

"Your father can tell you all about it," Nan said, kindly, not wishing to make Mr. Bulson any angrier. "He was there in the snowed-up train, too. That's how I came to be acquainted with your little dog. He was with your father on the train."

"Why, Pop!" cried the eager boy. "You never told me a word about it. And you must know this girl."

Mr. Ravell Bulson only grunted and scowled.

"What's your name, girl?" cried the boy, curiously.

"I am Nan Sherwood," the girl said, kissing him and then giving him a gentle push toward his father's outstretched and impatient hand. "If I don't see you again I shall often think of you. Be good to Buster."

"You must tell me about being snowed up, Pop," urged little Junior, as Nan turned away. "And I like that girl."

"That isn't much to tell—and *I* don't like her—nor any of her name," snapped Mr. Bulson.

"But you'll tell me about the snowed-up train?"

"Yes, yes!" cried his father, impatiently, anxious to get his lame son away from Nan's vicinity. "I'll tell you all about it."

Nan was quite sure that the fat man would be ashamed to give his little son the full particulars of his own experience on the stalled train. The little chap, despite his affliction, was an attractive child and seemed to have inherited none of his father's unhappy disposition.

"Good bye, Nan Sherwood!" he cried after the girl. "Come, Buster! Come, Buster! My, Pop! Buster likes that girl!"

"Well, I don't," declared the fat man, still scowling at Nan.

"Don't you?" cried Junior. "That's funny. I like her, and Buster likes her, and you don't, Pop. I hope I'll see you again, Nan Sherwood."

His father almost dragged him away, the spaniel, on a leash, cavorting about the lame boy. Nan was amazed by the difference in the behavior of Mr. Bulson and his afflicted son.

"And won't he be surprised when he learns that it wasn't Papa Sherwood, after all, but that wicked negro porter, who stole his wallet and watch?" Nan mused. "I hope they find the man and punish him. But—it really does seem as though Mr. Bulson ought to be punished, too, for making my father so much trouble."

Later "Nosey" Thompson *was* captured; but he had spent all Mr. Bulson's money in a drunken spree, and while intoxicated had been robbed of the watch. So, in the end, the quarrelsome fat man, who had so maligned Mr. Sherwood and caused him so much trouble, recovered nothing—not even his lost temper.

"Which must be a good thing," was Bess Harley's comment. "For if I had a temper like his, I'd want to lose it—and for good and all!"

"But there must be some good in that fat man," Nan said, reflectively.

"Humph! Now find some excuse for *him*, Nan Sherwood!" said her chum.

"No. Not an excuse. He maligned Papa Sherwood and I can't forgive him. But his little boy thinks the world of him, I can see; and Mr. Bulson is very fond of the little boy—'Junior,' as he calls him."

"Well," quoth Bess, "so does a tiger-cat love its kittens. He's a gouty, grumpy old fellow, with an in-growing grouch. I couldn't see a mite of good in him with a spyglass."

Her chum laughed heartily at that statement. "Well, let us hope he will keep so far away from us after this that we will have to use a spyglass to see him at all."

"And there's another person who can stay away from us," said Bess, suddenly.

"Who's that?" queried Nan, looking up at the change in Bess' voice.

"Linda Riggs. She's coming this way," Bess said, tartly.

This conversation occurred in the skating rink, and while Nan was having her skates strapped on by an attendant, for Walter Mason was not at the moment in sight.

The haughty daughter of the railroad president evidently proposed speaking with the chums from Tillbury. They had not seen her since the runaway and more than once Nan had wondered just what attitude Linda would take when they again met.

For Nan's part, she would rather not have met the rich girl at all. She had no particular ill-feeling toward her now; although time was when Linda had done all in her power to hurt Nan's reputation—and that not so very long past. But having actually helped to save the girl's life, Nan Sherwood could not hold any grudge against Linda. Bess, on the other hand, bristled like an angry dog when she saw Linda approach.

Linda came skating along warily, and arrived at the chums' bench by a series of graceful curves. She was rather a good skater, but more showy than firm on her skates.

"Oh, girls! I'm awful glad to see you," Linda cried, boisterously—and that boisterousness doubtless was assumed to cover her natural embarrassment at meeting again the girl whom she had so injured. "I didn't have time," pursued Linda, hurriedly, "the other day, to thank you properly—or Walter—for helping me out of that sleigh. I *was* scared."

"I should think you would have been," Bess said, rather grimly. "I'm sure I thought you would never get out of it alive."

"Well," repeated Linda, more doubtfully, for Nan had remained silent, "I wanted to thank you for what you did for me."

"You needn't thank me," said Bess, sharply. "For I didn't do a thing."

"Well, Nan Sherwood did, I s'pose," Linda observed, her color rising.

"You are heartily welcome if you think you need to thank me, Linda," Nan said, quietly. "But Walter really did it all."

"Of course!" said Linda, tossing her head, for Bess' manner had rasped the rich girl, "I know it took Walter to do it. But I presumed you girls expected to be thanked, too," and she turned sharply away.

"Oh, Bess! we ought not to have spoken as we did," murmured Nan, contritely.

"Pooh! Let her go. Mean old thing!" exclaimed Bess. "And you didn't say anything to get her mad. Crocodile tears! what did I tell you? Linda Riggs is a regular cat—"

"Both cat and crocodile?" giggled Nan. "Your natural history, Bess, honey, must be slightly twisted."

"I've about got that girl's number, just the same," said Bess, slangily. "You wait, Nan. She'll be just as mean when we get to Lakeview Hall as ever she was. Mark my word."

"All right, Worthy Prophetess," said Nan, seriously. "I mark thee well. But I am afraid we are in the wrong this time. We should have encouraged her attempt to be grateful."

She had no idea—nor had Nan Sherwood herself—that it lay within Linda's power, if it did in her wish, to injure Nan further. But Fate weaves strange webs of ordinary circumstances and that very evening Nan Sherwood came in close contact with Linda Riggs again, and the incident savored of a new peril, as keen as it was unexpected.

Walter was a minute late at the dinner table that night and as he slid into his seat beside Nan, after excusing himself to his mother and receiving her absolution in a smile, he whispered to Nan:

"What's 'on' for after dinner?"

"I really do not know of anything, Walter," she replied, smiling. "Don't you suppose we girls ever want to keep quiet? This visit to your house has been one continual round of pleasure—"

"Yes. You get *your* pleasure out of rescuing kids from the street, chasing runaway horses, hunting for runaway girls, and playing Sister of Charity to sick people. Say! your idea of pleasure, Nan Sherwood, is simply funny. Now, I've got something on for this evening, if you, and Bess, and Grace—and the kid, of course—want to go. But no crowd. My exchequer will not stand it.

"I'm running low in funds and father won't let *me* overdraw my allowance, although he lets Grace do it almost every month. He says a girl hasn't any head for figures, anyway, and she's to be excused."

"Oh, my!" gasped Nan. "That maligns the sex. I ought not to allow that, Walter Mason."

"Huh!" returned the boy, grinning. "Grace doesn't mind how much the sex is maligned, I warrant, as long as father hands her out an extra five whenever she runs short."

"But you haven't told me what the scheme is for this evening," Nan reminded him.

"Movies," Walter said. "There's a dandy new theatre opened on Halliburton Street. It isn't far, and mother approves of the class of pictures they run. There are going to be some funny ones shown to-night, too. I'll stand treat for you girls—but no more."

"Dear me, Walter," cried Nan. "You spend all your money on us girls."

"It couldn't go in a better cause," retorted the generous boy, stoutly.

Permission for the evening's outing was easily obtained, and the quintette of pleasure-seeking young folk hurried away immediately after dinner, so as to see the first show and get home early. Little

Inez was as eager and excited as she could be over the prospect of seeing a real movie show.

"I seen some pictures once in a dance hall where a man let me sell me flowers," she explained. "But, I never dared spend a nickel for no show. Me aunt would have scalped me—sure she would!"

Mr. Sherwood had seen Inez's aunt that afternoon, at his little daughter's request, and found that the woman dared make no objection as to their disposal of the child. In fact, she seemed a good deal relieved that kind friends had been raised for Inez.

The party arrived at the new picture palace to find a goodly crowd already assembled at the entrance. On this opening night there was a good deal of local interest shown, and the first picture was being finished when Nan Sherwood and her friends crowded into their seats.

"That's a good picture, I warrant," Walter said. "We want to stay and see that run over again. Ah-ha! here comes a Keynote Comedy. That will be a funny one, sure."

"I like to laugh," announced Inez, with her most serious air. "But I ain't never had much time for it."

"You poor little mite," said Bess. "I should say you hadn't. But you'll laugh all right when you get home with us to Tillbury. Won't she, Nan?"

"Of course she will," agreed Nan, squeezing the little one close to her.

They did not, however, laugh much at the picture which followed. The reels did not seem to run very evenly. Either the operator was not an experienced one or there was something the matter with the machine. The flash-card, "Wait a minute, please," appeared so frequently on the screen that the audience began to murmur, and some got up and went out.

There were others ready to take their places, and this continual changing of positions in the half-darkness of the house made a confusion that was hard to bear.

Nan and her friends moved over against the wall and another party came rustling in to take the seats in that row nearest to the aisle. Not

Nan Sherwood's Winter Holidays

until this crowd was seated did the party from the Mason house realize that it was anybody whom they knew.

Then Pearl Graves' rather loud voice broke in upon Nan and Walter's whispered conversation:

"Why! see who's here?" she cried. "Hullo, Walter Mason. Who's that you've got with you? Nan Sherwood, I'll be bound. And Grace, and Bess Harley. Hullo, girls! Is the show any good?"

"For goodness' sake!" interposed the sharp voice of the girl on the other side of Pearl. "Can't we go anywhere without running up against that Nan Sherwood and her crowd?"

"Oh, you be still, Linda!" laughed good-natured Pearl. "You ought to be pleased as Punch to see Nan and Walter. Between them they just about saved your life when Granny Graves' horses ran away with you the other day."

Little Inez was on Nan's other side and immediately Nan gave her attention to the child, leaving Walter free to talk with the newcomers if he chose.

"Did you like that picture, dear?" asked Nan of the little one.

"Hi! I liked it where the fat man slipped up on the soap at the top of the stairs and slid to the bottom where the scrub-woman left her tub of water. Do you 'spect that was *real* water, Nan Sherwood? He'd ha' been drowned, wouldn't he?"

"I guess it was real water," laughed Nan. "But they wouldn't let him be drowned in a picture."

"I forget it's a picture," sighed little Inez, exhibiting thereby true dramatic feeling for the art of acting. To her small mind the pantomime seemed real.

Another reel was started. The projection of it flickered on the screen until it dazzled one's eyes to try to watch it.

"Goodness!" gasped Pearl Graves. "I hope that won't keep up."

The excited little Hebrew who owned the theatre ran, sputtering, up the aisle, and climbed into the gallery to expostulate with the operator. There was an explosion of angry voices from the operator's box when the proprietor reached it.

The reel was halted again—this time without the projection of the usual "Wait a minute, please," card. The next instant there was another explosion; but not of voices.

A glare of greenish flame was projected from the box in the gallery where the machine was located—then followed a series of crackling, snapping explosions!

It was indeed startling, and there were a general craning of necks and excited whispering in the audience; but it might have gone no further had it not been for Linda Riggs.

It could not have been with malice—for the result swept Linda herself into the vortex of excitement and peril that followed; but the railroad president's daughter shrieked at the loudest pitch of her voice:

"Fire! fire! We'll all be burned to death! *Fire!*"

"Be still!" "Sit down!" were commands that instantly sounded from all parts of the house.

But the mischief was done, and Linda continued to shriek in apparently an abandonment of terror:

"*Fire! Fire!*"

Other nervous people took up the cry. Nearly half a thousand spectators were seated in the picture theatre and the smell of smoke was in their nostrils and the glare of fire above them.

For something, surely, was burning in the operator's box. The danger of the inflammable film was in the minds of all. A surge of the crowd toward the main exit signaled the first panic.

The outgoing rush was met by those who (not understanding the commotion) had been waiting at the back for seats. These people would not give way easily as the frightened audience pushed up the main aisle.

Those at the sides escaped more easily, for there was an exit on either side of the audience room. In the case of Nan Sherwood and her party, however, they were in the worst possible position as far as quick escape went. By some oversight of the fire inspectors the seats on several front rows had been built close against the sidewalls, with no passage at that end of the rows for entrance or egress.

Bess was next to the wall, and she jumped up, crying: "Oh, come on, girls! let's get out. Walter! I say, Walter! I'm frightened. Let us go."

Grace was crying.

Nan hugged Inez close to her and looked to Walter, too, to extricate them from their situation. But Linda had reached across her cousin, Pearl Graves, and clawed at Walter in abject terror. "Oh, save me! save me, Walter!" she moaned. "I am *so* afraid of fire—and in a place like this! Oh! oh!"

"Shut that girl's mouth!" exclaimed one man from the front. "Stop that screaming! There is no danger! The fire is confined to the box, and that is made of sheet iron. We're all right. Don't crowd!"

The panic had, however, spread too far.

The mob struggled and fought at the main doors. The police had been summoned; but they could not get into the building through the main entrance, and the side exits were toward the rear. Several people were knocked down and trampled on. A pungent odor of burning filled the theatre; the crackling of the flames grew louder and louder.

Walter had his hands full with Linda and Pearl, who had become likewise panic-stricken. Nan pushed Grace and Bess back toward the wall.

"Stand right where you are. We mustn't get in that crowd. We'll be killed," advised she, holding little Inez close to her.

"Save me! save me, Walter!" wailed Linda.

"I wish somebody would take this girl out of the way!" growled Walter Mason in much disgust, and far from gallant.

"Don't leave me!" shrieked Linda.

People began madly to climb over the seats—and over one another—to reach the side exits.

"How ever will we get out, Nan?" demanded Bess Harley, with keen faith in her chum.

"Keep still. Let us wait," urged Nan.

But at that instant red and yellow flames burst from the box where the picture projecting machine was housed. These flames began to lick up the furnishings of the balcony like so much tinder. Sparks and dense smoke were thrown off and both settled upon the struggling people below.

"Oh, Walter! Walter! We shall be burned," cried his sister.

The boy had never yet neglected his timid sister's cry. He somewhat rudely pushed Linda away and reached across Nan and Inez to seize Grace's hand.

"Pluck up your courage, Sis!" he cried, his voice rising cheerfully above the turmoil. "We'll get out all right."

"But *how*?" demanded Bess, in great anxiety. "Oh! see those sparks fly!"

"I see," said Nan, trying to speak calmly.

"They're falling right on those poor people—do, do look!" gasped Bess.

There was an open space between the young folks from the Mason house and the crowd that was wedged into the exit at the head of the main aisle. Upon this mob was pouring smoke and sparks. The flames ate up the bunting with which the balcony rail and pillars were decorated. The burning cloth floated down upon the heads of the excited people and threatened to set the dresses of some afire.

Pearl Graves had actually fainted in her seat. Linda lay across her cousin, sobbing and groaning. The rest of their party, whoever they were, had deserted the two girls.

"What under the sun shall we do, Nan?" whispered Walter, and Nan read the words on his lips rather than heard them; for the burning theatre was by this time a scene of pandemonium.

CHAPTER XXX

A FRESH OUTLOOK

Nan had already made up her mind what they must do. Despite the spread of the fire—and the heat of the flames already scorched their faces—she saw there was no escape for them by the front door of the building. And the chair-backs shut them off from the side exit.

"Get over the seat-back, Walter," Nan commanded. "Haul your sister and Bess over. I can climb over myself and take little Inez with me."

"Don't leave us to burn up!" shrieked Linda, wildly, starting up again. Her ears were keen enough.

"Pearl Graves has fainted," Walter said, hesitatingly.

"If we could only break down these seat-backs," cried Nan. "There are four rows between us and the side aisle."

"We *can* break them down," responded Walter, and immediately flung his weight against the back of the chair in which he had been sitting, glad to have some line of positive action suggested to him.

The boy's second attempt broke the back of the seat short off; it was built none too strong. He leaped over into the next row and quickly smashed his way through that.

"Come on, girls! I'll get you out," he cried, more cheerfully.

His sister and Bess climbed through the first aperture. Nan lifted Inez through and was about to follow, when Linda seized upon her jacket.

"You let me get out, Nan Sherwood!" she commanded, trying to pull Nan back.

"There is room enough—and time enough," panted Nan, resisting. "I must look after Inez."

"Let that young one go with Bess and Grace," Linda said. "Somebody's got to help me with Pearl. The silly has fainted."

Nan saw that this was so. She adjured Bess to take care of Inez.

"Hi! I don't need nobody ter take care o' me," cried that independent young lady. "I'm big enough to take care o' myself. You come on, Nan Sherwood."

"I'm coming," promised Nan, slipping back to help with Pearl.

Instantly Linda pushed by and followed the other girls, leaving Nan alone with Pearl Graves. The girl had no intention of helping her cousin.

Walter was smashing one seat-back after another, and calling to the girls to follow. Bess had grabbed up Inez and now only Nan and Pearl were left behind.

The latter was really senseless. Shaking her—patting her hands—rubbing her forehead—all did no good. It seemed impossible for Nan Sherwood to arouse her.

The smoke came down upon them, thick and stifling. The others of her party were shut out of Nan Sherwood's view. She heard them calling to each other, Walter shouting in advance. They thought Nan was coming, too.

Nan was dreadfully tempted to run. She was as frightened as she could be. She had a great terror of fire; ever since her experience with Cousin Tom in the forest fire, she had shuddered at the very thought of flames.

And here the heat of them almost overwhelmed her. The shrieks of the frantic throng at the main door of the theatre died away. She heard the shouted commands of the police and firemen—then the swish of water from the first pipe brought to play upon the flames. But they were all outside.

There was nobody near to help Nan Sherwood. She might easily have escaped by herself; but to leave this helpless girl whom Linda Riggs had abandoned—

Nan could not do that. She seized Pearl Graves by the shoulders and strove to drag her out of that row of seats and into the next. Although the main aide was now clear, she dared not try that way. Fire was raining down from the balcony into the back of the house.

Nan Sherwood's Winter Holidays

Pearl was a larger and heavier girl than Nan. Strong as the latter was, and well developed from her athletic training, the older girl would have been a heavy charge for Nan at best. Now, with the smoke half smothering her, and Pearl a dead weight in her arms, Nan could scarcely drag her burden to the opening in the row of seats.

She struggled to it, however, and got the girl through the first row of chairs, tearing Pearl's dress sadly in the effort and scratching her own ungloved hands. Nan was crying, too, as she struggled on; she was both frightened and unnerved.

But she stuck to her self-imposed task. She could hear no voices near her now. Nothing but the crackling of the flames and the crash of axes as the firemen wrecked the partition back of the balcony to get at the seat of the fire.

There was nobody to help Nan with her burden. A curtain of smoke shut off the firemen and policemen in the front of the house from the auditorium itself. The smoke grew thicker back there where the young girl struggled to reach the side exit.

Walter Mason and her other friends had escaped. Nan was glad of that. She did not even question why none of them came back to help her.

Nan did not know that the moment they appeared in the side alley, leading back to the rear of the theatre, a policeman with more zeal than good sense hustled them away from the door and would not let even Walter return when he found that Nan and Pearl were not with the party.

"Ye can't go back in there, me laddy-buck," declared the officer. "Is it crazy ye are? Phat's in that the-a-tre will have to stay there, if it can't git out be itself. Orders is ter let nobody inside."

"But something's happened to Nan!" cried Walter. "She and that other girl are perhaps overcome with the smoke. They'll smother!"

"Be still, I tell yez," commanded the officer, putting the boy back with one hand. "Orders is orders. Ye can't go back."

The situation quite overpowered Walter. He could not break through to help Nan and Pearl. His own sister was crying to him and begging him to come out of danger. Bess was screaming for Nan. Linda stood by, shaking with terror and cold. She doubtless realized that she had been the cause of the catastrophe.

And then, suddenly, little Inez broke away from Bess's restraining hand, and darted toward the exit, out of which the smoke was now pouring. Walter sprang forward again, too. The police officer caught the boy with a strong hand and hurled him back with an emphatic word; but Inez ran right between the officer's legs!

"Now, drat that young'un!" ejaculated the policeman, as Inez completely escaped him and disappeared under the pall of smoke.

"Oh, Inez! Come back! You'll be smothered!" shrieked Grace.

If the child heard this cry she paid no attention. Fearless and wild, she was too used to having her own way to obey now. And, besides, in her own queer, half-tamed way, she loved Nan Sherwood.

Being so tiny, Inez was less affected by the smoke than those who were taller. The blundering policeman who essayed to follow her into the doorway, came staggering back, choking and blinded. Walter himself, springing forward when he thought the way was clear, was met by the rolling volume of pungent smoke, which filled his lungs and stifled him.

"Come back! Come back, Walter!" wailed his sister.

With smarting throat and tearful eyes the boy obeyed—not because he wanted to. The heat and smoke overpowered him. The policeman was still choking and gasping.

Then, of a sudden, Bess Harley emitted an excited cheer. "Here they are! Hooray!" she shrieked.

Out of the doorway plunged little Inez, one arm over her eyes to defend them from the stinging smoke; one hand pulling at Nan's jacket, to guide her; for Nan came stumbling backward from the burning theatre, dragging Pearl Graves with her.

Both girls fell on the flagging as they reached the alley. The policeman and Walter raised Nan quickly. She did not lose consciousness; but she was scorched and breathless. Pearl, however, had not recovered her senses at all from the moment the shock had made her faint.

"She's—she's safe!" gasped Nan. "I covered her face so she should not breathe the smoke."

"And you're safe—you dear!" cried Bess, hugging her.

"And what a little trump that kid is," cried Walter, taking Inez by the shoulders and lifting her suddenly into his arms. He implanted a kiss on the child's smooched face, and put Inez down, laughing, when she struggled and cried out.

"Say, you're too fresh, you are," declared Inez. "Who told you you could kiss me? I don't like boys—much—anyway."

This made the other girls laugh. Walter aided Nan out of the alley. The policeman carried Pearl out into the back street and to the nearest drug store. There she was revived, and Linda telephoned for a taxi-cab to take them both home.

The rich girl had little to say to the Masons, or Nan and Bess. And certainly the four friends said nothing to her. They were convinced that there would have been no panic in the theatre had it not been for Linda Riggs; and her treatment of her own cousin had disgusted them all.

When Pearl had revived, being still very sick, the druggist gave her some medicine and then Linda took her home in the cab. Pearl knew, however, who had saved her from the fire. Bess Harley saw to it that there was no mistake about that.

"And we both owe our escape, I verily believe, to little Inez," Nan said, laughing, and stroking the head of the waif fondly. "The dear little thing came right inside and found us in the smoke. I was almost out of breath."

Pearl was quietly grateful to Nan, however, and she kissed Inez. When she went away in the cab Nan's hand was the last she touched, and Nan knew that she had made a friend for life of Pearl Graves. Nan refused to allow the Masons or Bess to talk of the matter. They all walked home, and by the time they reached the Mason house were all more quiet and able to appear before Mrs. Mason as though nothing extraordinary had happened.

It was not until the next morning at breakfast time, indeed, that Walter's and Grace's parents learned of the fire in the new theatre. Not much damage had been done the house; but several people had been hurt; and the escape of Walter and his party had been really miraculous.

"Goodness me!" sighed Mrs. Mason. "I shall be afraid to have you young folk out of my sight for the remainder of this vacation. What scrapes you manage to get into!"

These busy winter holidays were drawing to a close, however. Grace and Walter Mason and their two visitors, as well as all of their neighborhood friends, who had occupied themselves most enjoyably and in a dozen different ways, were now scattering for the latter half of the school year.

Nan did not see Linda Riggs again while she remained in Chicago. Immediately following the fire in the picture theatre, the railroad president's daughter went home. How she really felt toward Nan, the latter did not know; nor did this uncertainty bother her much.

Now that her father's trouble with Mr. Ravell Bulson was cleared up, Nan did not worry over anything but the seemingly total disappearance of the runaways, Sallie and Celia or, as they preferred to be known, Lola Montague and Marie Fortesque.

Mr. Sherwood was still in town to settle matters with the automobile company, and would return to Tillbury with Nan and Bess and Inez. Walter and Grace tried to crowd into the last forty-eight hours of the chums' stay all the good times possible, and the second night before Nan and Bess were to go home, a masquerade party was arranged at the Mason home. Of course, Mrs. Mason was the chief "patroness" of the affair and superintended the arrangements herself. So it was bound to be a success.

Nan needed some ribbons and a new pair of gloves at the last minute, and she ran out to get them herself. Trying shop after shop, just as the street lights were beginning to glimmer, she wandered some blocks away from the Mason house.

She reached a corner where there was a brilliantly lighted bakery beside a narrow and dark alley. Nan was looking for a shop where gloves were sold, not for a bakery; but some people coming out of the shop jostled her. She did not give the little group a second glance as they set off on their several ways from the bakeshop door.

Suddenly, she heard a voice say: "Oh, Sallie! they smell so good. I am as hungry as I can be."

Nan fairly jumped. She wheeled quickly to see two girls—one quite tall and pretty, after a fashion—standing with a bag of cakes between them. The tall girl opened it while the shorter peered in hungrily.

"Goodness! Can it be—?"

Nan's unspoken question was not completed, for out of the alley darted a street urchin of about Inez's age, who snatched the bag of cakes out of the girl's hand and ran, shrieking, back into the dark alley.

"Oh! the rascal!" gasped the taller of the two girls.

The other burst into tears—and they were very real tears, too! She leaned against the bakery wall, with her arm across her eyes, and sobbed.

"Oh, Marie, don't!" begged the other, with real concern. "Suppose somebody sees you!"

"I don't care if they do. And I *hate* that name,—Marie!" choked the crying girl, desperately. "I won't answer to it an—any more—so now! I want my own na—name."

"Oh, dear, Celia! don't be a baby."

"I—I don't care if I *am* a baby. I'm hun—hun—hungry."

"Well, we'll buy some more cakes."

"You can't—you shouldn't," sobbed the other, weakly. "I haven't any more money at all, and you have less than a dollar."

Nan had heard enough. She did not care what these girls thought of her; they should not escape. She planted herself right before the two startled strangers and cried:

"You foolish, foolish things! You are starving for greasy baker's cakes, when your fathers and mothers at home are just sitting down to lovely sliced ham and brown bread and biscuit and homemade preserves and cake—*and plenty of it all*! Sallie Morton and Celia Snubbins, I think you are two of the most foolish girls I ever heard of!"

The crying girl stopped in surprise. The other tried to assume a very scornful air.

"Haven't you made a mistake, Miss?" she said. "My name is Lola Montague and my friend is Miss Marie Fortesque."

"Sure they are," said the excited Nan. "I know they are your names, for you chose them yourselves. But I was at your house, Sallie Morton, the day of the big blizzard—the very day after you and Celia ran away. And if you'd seen how your mother cried, and how badly your father felt—

"And *your* mother is worried to death about you, Celia Snubbins; and your father, Si, who is a dear old man, said he'd give everything he owned to get you back—"

"Oh, oh!" gasped Celia, and burst into tears again.

"Listen to this, Sallie Morton!" added Nan, rummaging in her shopping bag and bringing forth Mrs. Morton's letter. She read some of the letter aloud to the girls.

"Now, Sallie, how dare you stay away from a mother like that? You've both just got to come with me. I should think you'd have found out by this time that neither of you will ever be famous as motion picture actresses."

"We have!" gulped Celia, plucking up a little courage. "You know we have, Sallie. That Mr. Gray told us to go back and milk the cows—you know he did!"

Sallie, determined as she was, was softened by her mother's letter. She said: "Well—if they'll have us back, I s'pose we might as well go. But everybody will laugh at us, Celia."

"Let 'em laugh!" cried her friend. "They won't laugh any harder than those folk in that studio did when we tried to act for the movies."

Their experience searching for work at the film studios all over Chicago had taught the two country girls something, at least. They had seen how poor people have to live in the city, and were going back to their country homes with an appreciation of how much better off they were there.

First, however, Nan forgot to buy her gloves; and instead took Sallie and Celia back to the Mason house with her. When she explained the situation to Walter and sent him out to telegraph to Mr. Morton, the boy laughingly nick-named the big Mason home, "The Wayfarers' Inn."

"If you stayed here a month longer, Nan Sherwood, you'd have the house filled with waifs and strays," he declared.

Sallie and Celia that evening divided interest with the masquerade party. The next day at noon, however, the fathers of the two girls arrived and took them home.

The farmers were grateful—loquaciously so on Mr. Si Snubbins' part—to Mr. and Mrs. Mason for housing the runaways over night; but neither could properly express the feeling he had for Nan Sherwood.

Mrs. Morton did that later in a letter, and Nan keeps that much-read letter to this very day in the secret box in which she locks her medal for bravery. She thinks a great deal more of the letter from the grateful farmer's wife than she does of the Society's medal.

Before Nan Sherwood returned to Tillbury she saw Jennie Albert again, and finally made a special call upon Madam, the famous film actress, to beg that kind, if rather thoughtless, woman, to take the girl under her own special and powerful protection.

Inez went to Tillbury and Mrs. Sherwood welcomed the waif just as Nan knew she would. While Nan was absent at school, her mother would have somebody to run errands and who would be cheerful company for her in "the little dwelling in amity."

So we leave Nan Sherwood, looking toward her second term at Lakeview Hall, and about to renew her association with the girls and instructors there—looking forward, likewise, to hard study, jolly times, and a broadening opportunity for kindly deeds and pleasant adventures in her school life.

Copyright © 2023 Esprios Digital Publishing. All Rights Reserved.